Dangerous F
© Steven For

Opening

The recently polished motorbike would stay where it was this morning. The young fella fancied stretching his legs. He also fancied that some fresh air might help him deal with the hangover.

The one and only Rudy Rudge, too cool for school, too hot to handle, every school girl's wet dream, strutted down North Parade. As he passed the old County Hotel a brief feeling of sadness passed over him. All boarded-up it was a sorry sight. But the feeling soon passed as he carried on towards Grand Parade.

Friday meant two things in Rudy's world. Pay day and *Lush night*. Lush was Skegness's premier nightclub. Rudy and his mate Pez would be hitting the dance floor later on with one thing on their minds!

As the kid was about to reach work he looked at his phone and saw that he had a message from his mum. He hadn't spoken to her in more than a week (and hadn't seen her in a fortnight). This was not the usual 'hi, how are you'. Something was wrong. She said she needed to see him in person as soon as he could *spare the time*. His old dear lived over at Paxton Fields (the old family home) with her partner Ravi. Rudy didn't much like him.

The only son of Cyril & Dora Rudge wasn't so keen on putting a downer on his Friday night. He had a mind to go and see mum tomorrow after he had blown off some steam.

The kid walked into the Plaza ten minutes early for his shift and saw that his colleague Kai was busy getting the place up and running. He could hear his boss talking to some delivery guy in the back.

"Another day in paradise" Rudy said to the baby woman. She told him he looked rough and followed up by telling 'the one and only' to make himself useful. He pulled a face before turning to the nearest change dispenser.

Rudy liked the smell of the place at this time of day. The air felt crisp even inside. It never lasted long. By midday all of the old regulars would be in their usual spots. The kid didn't feel so bad for any of them. These old timers in their 'cabbage cars' were right where they wanted to be. If folks wanted to fritter away their benefits in the warm neon glow of the Plaza, pulling on the handle of a fruit machine or frantically tapping away on red and yellow square buttons, that was A OK with Rudy. It was better than ok actually.

These Skegness legends were putting money in his pocket and a dubious smile on his boss's face.

Clinton Klein was the man who owned the gaff. He told Rudy that he'd won the place from a Dutchmen in a poker game. Of course this was bullshit and everyone knew it. This was the answer Klein would give to his employees if they were curious to ask how long he'd been 'the man' here.

Klein was of Dutch birth but he'd lived in Lincolnshire most of his life. Rudy had heard rumours that he'd spent some time in prison. Depending on who you spoke to it was fraud or tax evasion or cocaine dealing. People in Skeggy could never get their stories straight. Usually Clinton would come out and banter with the staff a bit but today he stayed in his office.

Rudy was an attendant. 30 hours a week for

little more than minimum wage. The regulars liked him for three reasons. He was quick to bring drinks around when asked, he never gave them any shit about their language or occasional aggressive behaviour, and he knew how to fix the machines when they were playing up. They often were playing up so Rudy had to stay on his toes.

There were three reasons why Kai wasn't too keen on her colleague. The first being that he was impulsive. Secondly, he appeared to let his dick do most of his thinking (never a good thing). And thirdly, he over estimated his intelligence as many guys do (young and old). Even so, she had to admit that he did have redeeming qualities. Rudy was generous. He had lent her money more than a few times without asking why she needed it. She could see he wasn't a cruel sort. That made him stand out a little from the crowd of adolescents that would sometimes swarm into the place and make her life harder than it otherwise would have been.

Just as business was kicking into that higher gear by mid afternoon in came Rudy's old man Cyril. His dad's face was a couple of shades darker than when he had seen him just a few hours ago. He had bad news.
He didn't explain much but Rudy knew from what little he did tell him that tonight's festivities would have to be postponed. He was being told that he had to go over to his mum's as soon as his shift finished.
When six o'clock did come around the young fella headed off towards Paxton Fields with a palpable sense of dread drowning out his frustration.

Part One: R.I.P but life goes on

Ravi's face looked as grim as Cyril's did

earlier. Rudy rudely pushed past him and started calling after his mother. He found her sat in the living room. She had clearly been crying. Her eyes were blood shot and her cheeks were puffy. "What's happened then" the kid said, his voice trembling a little. Dora looked past him into the garden. The grass was less green today. She asked her son to sit down. This made him more nervous. "Your uncle Leonard has died. They found him yesterday. From what little they've told me..." Dora paused to light a cigarette. As she exhaled and closed her eyes Rudy felt his whole body tense up. He thought she was about to tell him that his uncle had been murdered. "It looks like he went and hung himself". Dora looked at her son expecting to see a stunned boy staring back at her. But Rudy looked to the corner of the room. She read confusion and disgust on his face. The woman rose from her chair and moved to sit

next to Rudy. She gave the lad's back a tender rub as she offered him a smoke.
Ravi came and stood in the doorway. He mouthed the words "you ok?" to his partner. Dora nodded. "Your dad's coming over in a bit darling. He'll bring us all something from the chippy. Maybe we'll have a few drinks later A son?"
Rudy needed a moment alone. The heat in the living room had suddenly become almost suffocating. Again he pushed past Ravi. The lad headed out into the garden to pull in some deep breaths. His stomach churned as his heart sank. The sound of a happy child playing with a dog nearby brought a couple of tears rolling down his cheeks.

Half an hour or so after Rudy had arrived his old man showed up with some food and a couple of bottles of wine.
At the kitchen table his parents talked about

the latest goings on in town. The two main topics of conversation doing the rounds this week were Council taxes going up, which of course negatively effected lower income people more so than the middle classes, and a fire that had broken out at the Nutlins resort in Ingoldmells. Rumors were swirling that it might have been arson. Ravi said that he'd heard it might have been the work of a disgruntled employee. "There's every chance it was just an accident" Cyril countered. "They don't have a great safety record there mate".

The four of them sat watching the telly into the night. Once Rudy had gotten a couple of drinks in him he perked up a little. But Dora could see that this was hitting him hard. She too was hurting of course. She had just lost her big brother in the most awful of ways. The next few days would be dark. She would have to make several very hard phone calls. There was the funeral to think about. Of course the police would have to complete their investigation first and then there would be the post mortem exam. As this was a suicide there would have to be an inquest. All of this would be stressful.

The wheels of the system turn slowly. Dora knew this. After her father died it took more than six months for everything to be sorted out.

Rudy woke up on Saturday morning feeling a wee bit rough. He wasn't used to drinking red wine. He had slept at his mum's in his sister's old room and had woken early. He knew his mother would have already left for work so it would have been just him and Ravi in the house. The young fellow didn't want to have any interactions with his old dear's boyfriend so he shot out of the door a minute after he had cleaned his teeth. There was no work for the 'one and only today' so he headed back towards North Parade. Though he tried to push it out of his mind he couldn't stop thinking about Leonard. His Uncle lived in Boston. Rudy would have last seen him about a month ago at his mum's. He seemed like he was in good spirits on that day (a Saturday under clear blue skies not unlike this one). He didn't know his uncle too well. He was that family member he would see from time to time. He was generous and clearly liked a drink. He enjoyed the company of others from what Rudy could tell. Why would this cheerful bloke do himself in? The kid was finding it hard to believe.

Once he got clear of town on his Yamaha 125 he found that his mind began to clear. Being on the bike helped him to focus on the moment. When you're tearing down the A52, really opening up the throttle, you have to be present. The lad went all the way down to Boston. When he reached the outskirts of town he stopped and considered his options. A small part of him wanted to carry on towards Skirbeck so he could ride past Leonard's gaff. What good would this do though? As the youngster sat on his black & blue pride & joy he saw a middle aged man walking past the Premier Inn with a pink t-shirt that caught his eye. In block white capitals were the words 'I BEAT MY KIDS DEBATE ME'. Why such a shirt would exist Rudy didn't know. His hard laughter remained hidden under his helmet. After he had recovered he headed up towards Sibsey village. Then he headed west on Station Road back towards the A52. He was definitely feeling better as he came ripping back into Skeggy.

It was almost always the same routine after a

ride. The bike went back in the same spot. He dismounted and stood on the path looking at 'Tawny' (this being the name of his mechanical girlfriend). He would crouch for a little bit, checking over the tyres and the engine. He wasn't really checking so much as he was admiring. He would do this for several minutes. One of his neighbours, Mrs Green, watching out of the window as she did the washing up, thought him quite strange. From her perspective it looked like he was in a trance.

As he was struggling with his front door key his old man opened up. 'Where did you go bud?" Cyril asked. Rudy fiddled with the visor on his helmet and stepped through the doorway. "Just went for a run up to Mablethorpe".

Back in his bedroom Rudy sat in his swivel chair as the old laptop went through its loading procedure. He was troubled by what he had just done. *Why did I just lie to the old man? There wasn't any good reason for it.* The young fella heard the front door open and close. He rolled his chair to the window to confirm what he already knew. Off went his dad towards town.

For his father Saturday was just like any other day. Cyril had been unemployed for the better part of ten years. He had worked in the pub & restaurant trade for a good while after his school days. He was pretty good at his job and was well liked by colleagues and regulars.

In his early thirties he did his back in while lifting a beer keg. He had hoped that after a couple of weeks rest he would have been all healed up. But unfortunately some permanent damage had been done. His doctor had been less than helpful. The local GP had just tried to push some pills off on him.

He went to see a specialist who made some basic recommendations and then sent him off for some physiotherapy. This helped but not a great deal.

His boss was a good guy and very understanding about the situation. He offered him reduced hours which he took for a while, but the pain of working even a 30 hour week became too much. He soon found out that he could pull in more income on welfare than he could suffering behind the bar so the choice was an easy one.

Around town Cyril was a face that most of the locals knew. He liked to get a pint or two in him but he wasn't a drunk. He enjoyed a bet on the football and the horses but he didn't have a gambling problem. He could be seen walking slowly up and down Skegness's long sandy beach on a sunny afternoon staring out at the calm sea. He enjoyed being a man of leisure. Even so, he felt as if he were guilty somehow. Like it was his fault he injured himself. This was simply not true but the negative thoughts remained. He also blamed himself for the break up of his marriage. It was more reasonable here to say he shared culpability with Dora for the failed relationship. The pair had separated when Rudy was just 12 (and his sister Geraldine was 15). In every marriage people will find things they don't like about each other. People will find faults and reasons to complain and argue. Like many working class folks Dora and Cyril didn't make life easier for themselves when things got heated. They never really learned any conflict resolution skills. They would find ways to hurt each other with their words and tone. Some things once said...

Rudy knew his dad would be out and about

for several hours. The kid looked at his phone and saw that he had a couple of messages from Pez asking what he was up to (and asking 'how shit was going'). Rudy told him that he would text him later when he was about to come over and tell him all about it in person. The young man then turned his phone off and drew the curtains.

A little private time meant Rudy could indulge in fantasy and, in the process, let his mind escape from the troubles and stress of the moment.

One of his *go to* websites was called *heavy mother*. It was basically a porn site for people with more extreme tastes in either the sadistic or masochistic direction. Rudy was a masochist. Why this was he didn't know and didn't particularly care. He knew what he liked. That's what mattered.

A few days ago he had come across a video in

which a young woman with strawberry blonde hair (dressed in thigh high leather boots and little else) was doing a POV (point of view) routine in a dungeon of some kind. The fantasy situation was basically; she had captured the viewer (having tricked him into helping her in some way with the old damsel in distress routine) and now she had *you* tied to a chair naked and was about to *complete her conquest*. This would involve riding the viewer while slowly cutting off his oxygen supply with a belt (until death).

Rudy sat naked in his swivel chair (pushed right back up against his bed). With his right hand he pumped his dick. With his left he pulled his purple necktie tighter and tighter around his throat. He had plenty of practice getting the timing right. As the video neared its conclusion he achieved an intense release. As he ejaculated his left hand loosened its grip. He resisted the urge to pull in a big breath. The lad came pretty close to passing out. He looked down at the crimson carpet in his room, his ears ringing. The dopamine hit was obscene. He would sit there and enjoy it for a good five minutes before getting up to clean the mess.

Rudy's best mate Pez also lived on North Parade. Like his bud he had spent his entire life in Skegness. He shared his friend's love of motorbikes. At school they had bonded over this. Both lads had found themselves in the lower sets for most of the main subjects at the Academy coed.

Pez (real name Lee Peston), even as a young teenager, had accepted that he wasn't so sharp in the academic sense and as such his prospects would be limited. He wasn't wrong. For Rudy it was different. He just never really applied himself at school. There was no teacher that really inspired or lit a fire under him. Both friends managed to stay out of trouble (for the most part) until their older teenage years.

Early Saturday evening saw Rudy and Pez getting a few beers in them prior to a night out at Lush (Skeggy's premier nightclub). He had told his bud all about what had gone on yesterday as soon as he had come around. Lee didn't know how to react. His friend didn't seem to be too cut up about it though. Rudy said "you never really know what's going on in someone's head do you? The thing is, he was a cheerful bloke. I just don't get it man. Something don't add up". Pez had questions forming in his mind but he resisted the voice telling him to ask. Instead he simply offered his condolences and said they should drink to his uncle's memory and have a good time tonight.

The lads were pleased to find that there

wasn't too big of a queue when they arrived outside just after seven. Pez was wearing his eye catching orange shirt and had slicked his hair back as he often did on a night out. Rudy was wearing one of his black polo neck tops with matching dark trousers. Pez teased him sometimes when he wore the darker gear, saying that he looked like a keyboard player from an 80's synth band.

The boys didn't need to flash their I.D's as the bouncer knew them well. As soon as they were inside they headed for Custers, which was the pub section of the club. Lush was set over several floors. In one part you had Custers pub/bar, in another you had the main dance floor. On the second floor you had a fancy cocktail bar. And on the third deck was the function rooms for private parties. One part of the Custers pub was sectioned off from the rest of the bar area. This was for the karaoke. This area was quiet early on in the night but by eleven it would surely be full of piss heads belting out ballads from years gone by.

It took Rudy and Pez longer to get to the bar than it did to get into the club. Custers was fairly packed. They ordered a couple of pints of Gusto and turned to face the revelers.

Pez began nudging his mate and pointing out a few *fit birds* close by.

In Custers they would see plenty of *local talent*. Some of the Skegness ladies could be seriously rowdy. The university crowd was a different sort to the locals though. Saturday would bring young ladies over from Lincoln, some of whom might not have set foot in Skeggy before. Sometimes you would get (what Rudy and Pez would call) *posh foreign sorts* in Lush. Trying it on with them could be challenging but fun.

Mr Rudge liked to think he had a good eye for picking out girls who would be game.

Tonight he could already see that he was spoiled for choice.

Rudy was going to take his time. He had his first target in his sights but was in no rush to go over and introduce himself. Pez by contrast had already left his mate at the bar and was chewing the ear off of a local hairdresser by the name of Gemma. She wasn't entirely repulsed by the young buck (indeed she knew him from previous encounters in the club and elsewhere) but his chances of *pulling* this lass were not great. Rudy kind of enjoyed watching his friend go to work (and fail as he did most of the time). Pez was not the sort who let rejection get to him too much. He never really let the knock backs get him down. With Rudy it could go either way. If a girl made it clear that she wasn't liking his approach work from the start he was better able to walk away and not dwell on it. However, if he sensed that a girl was leading him on, flirting and giving him signals, only to turn her back and focus attention on someone or something else, then he could get upset.

He waited until the girl was alone. She stood near to the toilet door fiddling with her fingers. She had just separated from her friends. The kid took the direct approach as he often did. He introduced himself with a kindly smile and told her she looked very beautiful. He took her off guard. This was good.
The lady had short red hair and was wearing a low cut white dress. When he asked her name he was half expecting to hear a foreign accent but instead it was a very middle class English voice which introduced herself as Ivy. "I don't think I've ever met an Ivy before" said Rudy, still smiling. She had a soft

feminine voice and a sweet round face with brown eyes. The lad thought that she couldn't be older than 18. He wasn't about to ask her age. He was about to offer the lady a drink when her two friends came out of the toilet and came over as if to rescue Ivy from the keen young fellow in the polo neck. "I'm going to see you for a dance later on Ivy... right?" The girl smiled at Mr Rudge as she was whisked away. He could tell that there was a chance for him with this one. It was a pleasant surprise that the first girl he spoke to seemed to be game. And she was a *posh* sort.

Rudy was careful not to get too pissed early on. He tried chatting up another girl in the bar but she clearly wasn't into what he was selling.

He could tell that his partner in crime was not having much luck tonight. Perhaps his fortunes would change when they hit the dance floor later.

By ten the floor was starting to fill out with hungry young bodies. It was clear from the way things were kicking off that the MDMA dealers were having a good evening. Rudy & Pez weren't into that scene but they were not above taking advantage of girls feeling the effects of Ecstasy.
The lad watched Ivy and her friends throwing some shapes as the base pounded out, making the room vibrate. He was going to slide up beside her when the moment was right.

The lad woke up in his clothes at just after eleven. He had slept through three alarms. The old man came knocking at his door just as he was getting changed into his work threads. "Good night bud?" Rudy managed to force out a "yeah...it was alright". Cyril couldn't tell what kind of mood his son was going to be in today. He offered to make him some tea and toast. The kid wanted a coffee. He must have only gotten five hours of sleep tops. Even so, as he walked towards Grand Parade, taking in the sights and sounds, he felt wide awake and in good form.

Sunday could be a slow start at the Plaza. That suited our young man just fine. Kai and Rudy were joined today by a lad named Eric. This boy was what Mr Rudge called an emo. During one conversation they were having a couple of weeks ago Eric had said that he wished he could 'turn his feelings off and on like a tap' as this would make his life flow more easily. This was pure emo talk in Rudy's mind. He found it amusing but resisted the urge to take the piss.

Clinton was out of the door almost as soon as they had opened up. He looked to be in a hurry wherever it was he was going.

Kai knew she was going to hear about

Saturday night at Lush before things got busy. From her colleague's cheerful demeanor she thought he would be telling her about his latest conquest. Instead she heard 'the one and only' go into some detail about being 'cock blocked' by the friends of *the object of his affections.*
That he described the girl in such a way that did nothing to concealed his lust was of no surprise. But there was more to it. He said this Ivy was a bit of class and that she was *captivating.* Kai had never heard him use such a word. She wondered if he might have taken something last night. He was pleased with himself clearly. He had managed to find out that she was a student at the University of Lincoln and he had managed to get a phone number despite the girl's friends best efforts to shoo him away.
He was confident that he would see her again in the club. Next time she wouldn't get

away from him.

With some of the regulars wheeling on in through the entrance Rudy's attention started to focus on the present. Kai was glad of this. If he kept talking it was going to get on her nerves.

It was a trouble free shift right up until the last hour. At five o'clock in through the entrance came Bobby Rees. His little brother Doug was with him and another couple of shifty looking youths made up the group. Bobby had been banned from the Plaza after he had punched one of the regulars following an altercation. He had it fact been banned from three other arcades on the Parade for similar violent offenses.

Rudy thought that Rees might be here looking for Clinton. It was the boss who had thrown the delinquent out on his ear back in March. But Clinton was not around this time.

It would surely fall on Rudy to do something when called for.

For about twenty minutes Bobby and his mates amused themselves playing on the old Supreme Fighter retro game. It was when the group leader starting doing some moves IRL on his brother that things started kicking off. Bobby got his sibling in a head lock and wrestled him to the floor. The kid started squealing loudly which drew the attention of everyone in the place. Kai and Eric looked to Rudy to intervene as he knew they would. "Alright girls. Time to do one yeah. You know you're not allowed in here anyway". The fifteen year old wannabe tough guy let go of his brother and squared up to the attendant. He saw no trace of fear in the man's eyes. Rudy leaned in close to the boy and almost whispered "try something you little cunt". The other lads heard what Mr Rudge said and began to back away. They guessed from the

look on his face that he wasn't kidding.
Bobby Rees smiled at the fella who had just threatened him. He had just earned his respect. Still smiling (in a creepy way) the dickhead departed the scene, taking his little crew of idiots with him.

Rudy felt pretty good about himself as he went around to check up on the regulars. He was complimented for the way he dealt with 'those dumb twats'.

Around town there were at least ten Bobby Rees's. Rudy, in his capacity as an arcade attendant, had never had to get physical but he felt it was only a matter of time. He was confident that he could take care of a jumped up scruff like Rees or anyone like him.

After the work day was done young Mr Rudge headed over to Pez's to tell him about the little bit of excitement that had happened earlier at the Plaza. He found his mate in a good mood. "I'm getting a new bike! Saw it today round at Shane's gaff". The bike he referred to was a second hand 125. Mr Peston had sold his old wheels more than a month ago and was eager to get back out on the road. The pair could go riding together again. A trip up to Scarborough was suggested. Naturally this made Rudy think of his sister. Geraldine had lived up there with her partner for more than three years. It had been perhaps six months since he had dropped by. He knew his parents would be going up soon enough anyway (to talk about Leonard of course). Maybe he would see Gerry first.

The morning of the funeral proved to be a tense affair. There was no wake in the traditional sense.
Naturally Dora found the day to be emotionally challenging from the moment

she got up and this wasn't helped by the atmosphere being created by her partner and ex-husband. Cyril and Ravi could get on each others nerves sometimes. Today was one of those times. Both men felt it was their role to be there as the support Dora needed. Neither was wrong but they were both going about it in the wrong way. The unneeded competitiveness bothered Rudy and Geraldine also.

Just prior to leaving the house to go to the Church Dora said a few words to both men, hoping it would cause some self-reflection. It caused some face pulling.

In the car she sat next to her son and held his hand. The old amber coloured Ford Fiesta crawled slowly behind the black hearse.

On the journey over to St Clements Rudy found that his thoughts were on his mother rather than his late uncle. In the days leading up to this he had been thinking about

Leonard and why he did what he did. It had taken the kid a while to accept it probably was suicide. But a part of him was still pushing back against his better judgment. The young man was glad that his sister was present. Gerry was a calming influence on their parents. She knew how to handle the old man in stressful situations and she had a way with her mother that Rudy appreciated and was perhaps a little envious of.

Immediate family and two close friends listened to the vicar speak of a man who didn't sound too familiar. The large blown up photo of Leonard just to the left of his coffin must have been taken more than 10 years ago. It wasn't a flattering shot.
When it was Dora's time to speak the guys and Geraldine were more than a bit concerned about her state of mind. She had burst into tears twice today and appeared to

be shaky and somewhat spaced out.

She hadn't prepared anything to read. There was no need. Dora held it together as she spoke of the lad her brother once was growing up in the 1980's and 90's. She painted the picture of a caring and kind hearted young fella who was protective of his sibling. She made it clear that he was the one she leaned on after the passing of their mother at a relatively young age (due to the ravages of alcoholism). She told the small gathering in no uncertain terms that her brother was a good man. He would be truly missed.

Rudy was proud of his mum. She had paid her tribute beautifully. What a tragic thing it was that this man had taken his own light and put it out forever.

At the Seathorne Arms, just down the road from the Nutlins resort, the family gathered.

Leonard's old mates Dave and Jim came along to join them for a couple of drinks and a slap up meal. Of course these gents wanted to talk about 'Lenny' and what a stand up fella he was. Dora welcomed their stories. Her brother had been well liked at work. She heard that he, one of the lower level bosses on the factory floor, was a guy the young ones felt comfortable coming to when they were having problems. Another chap in a similar position of authority was apparently not so well liked or respected (Dave and Jim clearly thought he was a bit of a cunt). The guys admitted that Lenny had covered for them on more than one occasion and had been generally lenient when he didn't need to be. Those present at the table got the impression that these two blokes might not be working for Lincolnshire Tyres Inc for much longer.

After everyone had got a fair bit of alcohol in

them the conversation drifted away from the dearly departed. The subject of the Nutlins fire came up. Ravi talked excitedly about the arrest of an employee (who had yet to be named). The story had been covered in the local papers and many thought the national tabloids would get a hold of it soon enough. Rudy wondered if the culprit might be someone he knew or even went to school with.

When Dave and Jim went on their way Dora and Cyril told the pair to stay in touch. Rudy's mum gave them both an extra long hug. Young Mr Rudge didn't think they would be seeing very much of either one again. They would return to their lives in Boston. Leonard would become a sad memory of the way things used to be. Rest in Peace but life goes on.

Rudy and his sister slept over at their mum's

that night. Gerry was back in her old room and young Mr Rudge was down in the living room in his old sleeping bag. With the curtains drawn it was almost pitch black. His restless mind went over the events of the day. The social interactions of the last twelve hours played out in the dark. His dad and Ravi seemed to cool off and get along much better by the time they had imbibed a few drinks. His mother was raw and honest with everyone she spoke with. She had wore her heart on her sleeve where others had remained more reserved. Rudy had caught a few little glances from his sister in Church and in the pub afterwards. It was rare to see her look at him in that way. She had looked into him rather than at him. His thoughts lingered on her as he drifted off to the land of nod.

Shooting straight off without saying where

he was going would worry his parents for sure. The kid woke up in a funny kind of mood. Twenty minutes of power walking didn't put him in a better frame of mind. On North Parade outside his gaff his saw two choices before him. He could have gone inside and indulged in one of his lurid fantasies. But with the day looking good and clear as it did and with Tanwy just sat there making eyes at him as she did...

On the way up to Scarborough just recently he had seen Pez almost get taken out at a crossroads by a work truck. It didn't scare him. It should have.

The kid was making some dangerous moves. He was good. He was good and he knew it. He knew how to move his bike around and shift himself almost expertly at this stage. He'd been riding bikes since he was eleven. In that time he'd had a few falls as everyone who rides did. He broke his ankle when he was fourteen in one particularly bad spill. This one happened on an old recreation ground a few miles south of Skeggy. Fortunately Pez and another lad were there at the time. Rudy could still remember being in the hospital shortly after the accident. The smell of the place never left him. As is fairly typical of young guys he fell in love with the nurse who was treating him. He could recall how concerned his mum and dad were. They split up two years previously but this incident did bring them together again (if only for a brief period of focused parental worry).

What did Rudy take from his broken ankle? The pain was just temporary. The experience of being out of control like that, flying over the handlebars, the mind in complete panic, that was <u>raw life</u>. That was life at the living end.

He took Tawny as far as Woodhall Spa. Here he stopped to stretch his legs and give his neck and shoulders a rub and a crack. He briefly entertained the idea of going on to Lincoln but decided to head home. He rode back towards the coast as if he were trying to beat his time getting over to the quaint little town (which like a lot places in Lincolnshire looked like it was stuck firmly in the past).

He was fully aware that the way in which he rode left him 2 seconds from disaster at almost every turn. He knew he was playing a dangerous game. He knew that somewhere else in the Country today, someone like him, would be having their lifeless body scrapped off the road because he made a bad call or just had some real bad luck. Too bad for that guy.

Back in his room Rudy was able to find a moment of calm. But when he turned his phone back on the moment was lost. Several angry family members wanted a word or two.

When he finally got around to calling her he wondered if he'd perhaps left it too late. But the kid was delighted to find the little fire cracker who had caught his eye that night in Lush was coming back to Skeggy. Rudy was less delighted to hear she was coming back with her friends. And this time they were not going to the club. They were going to watch a psychedelic rock band called *Planet Exploder* at the Red Lion. Young Mr Rudge was more than a little amused. When he told Pez about this later on they both had a good belly laugh about it. Saturday was shaping up to be an interesting night.

On Friday at work Rudy, Kai and Eric were all starting to get somewhat concerned by the boss's behaviour. Recently he had been absent more than usual and when he was in the back he would keep locking the door (with the *do not disturb* sign displayed prominently). Kai quietly suggested that he might be in some legal or financial trouble. Eric floated the notion that gangsters or money lenders could be after him. Rudy knew that this was just idle speculation but he wasn't about to offer any words of caution.

"I suppose you and your boy will be tearing it up at Lush tomorrow then?" Kai asked the question as she peered towards the entrance. "No. Bit of a change of pace actually...Red Lion". Clearly Mr Rudge's answer had caused some surprise. "Get out of town! Me too. You're going to watch the band?" Rudy smiled and then started chuckling a little. "What's funny?" Kai waited for a reply but got none. Instead Rudy called Eric over. "Are you going to the Red Lion tomorrow buddy?" The lad confirmed that he was. "Well, this should be fun A folks". Kai gave her smirking colleague a suspicious look. "There's a girl isn't there? I don't think I've ever seen you in the Lion on a Saturday night". 'The one and only' kept wearing his smirk as he went about his duties.

Over a couple of bottles of lager around at Rudy's the boys went over a little game plan prior to stepping out onto the Parade. Rudy wanted Pez to act as a distraction figure of sorts when he gave the signal. The goal would be to separate Ivy from her cock blocking pals. Young Peston was on board. The idea of fucking with a couple of posh sorts to help his mate out sounded like fun. When the lads arrived the Lion was teeming with local stoners and emo kids. Music nights at pubs like this could pull in the kind of people some locals might label as weird or queer.

Things didn't start too well. The lads were jostled as they tried to make their way to the bar. Rudy reacted quite badly to this. He shoved a young bleach blonde guy which caused his mates to push back at Mr Rudge. Pez managed to act as peace maker, moving his buddy away from the trouble. This put a little black cloud over the kid's head for a bit but he soon forgot about it when he saw Ivy's beaming smile. She looked fantastic in her gold dress with white shoulder straps. Her friends were either side of her.
Rudy and Pez put their heads together and came up with a couple of plays as they supped their beers. Pez would make his move first.

'The one and only' was very happy to see that his partner in crime was making a scene. Ivy's taller mate in the short green skirt seemed to be getting quite hot under the collar. Mr Peston could be really annoying when he put his mind to it. When he switched his attention to Ivy's other friend Rudy made his move. He swiftly weaved in and out of the weirdos and came up behind the gorgeous lady. He gently put his hand on her shoulder which made the girl jump a wee bit. When he was greeted by that lovely smile he melted somewhat (causing him to almost forget his opening line).

Just as he was finding his feet and turning on the charm the curtain around the small stage area came up to reveal Planet Exploder. Some enthusiastic whooping ensued.

The four member group took no time with the set up. Their lead singer, a long haired dude in a Fink Floyd t-shirt who looked like he'd just rolled out of bed, introduced himself as Travis Stallone. Just this in itself almost caused Rudy to burst out laughing. Between Ivy and the band, Rudy had almost forgotten about his mate. When he turned around to see where Pez was pub security had him in the corner (giving him a stern talking to by the look of it). Ivy's protectors were however still distracted. They had started a conversation with a couple of goth girls. All four of them were looking in the direction of Pez and security.

Planet Exploder were everything Rudy wanted them to be. Clearly these lads had grossly overestimated their musical abilities. The opening song was about exploding across the galaxy to escape conformity or some such shite. It was awesomely bad and he was loving it. Ivy too was clearly into it. Rudy was going to wait until the third or forth tune and then make his move. He didn't have to make any moves. Just as the second slammer of a track started Ivy moved her hand between his legs and gave his 'little brother' a squeeze. She gave him the look. He wanted to move in for a kiss but something stopped him. She then gave him the eyebrow as she faced back towards the small stage.

It was a sound night out on the whole. The only downer had been that his main man had been ejected from the Lion. Rudy tried to put this out of his mind. It wasn't so hard. Now he had Ivy alone.

The looks on the faces of her friends as they exited the pub, not long after Planet Exploder had finished their set in *epic* style, was priceless. As far as the kid was concerned he had won the night.

As he and the English Literature student walked towards his place it became increasingly clear that he was dealing with a real wit. She was confident and well spoken. She was playful and cheeky.

He could tell that he was making a decent impression on her. She was liking his cocky manner.

The old man had gone to bed. Rudy could see that he hadn't bothered to clean up after himself in the living room. This was common on a Saturday. The lad didn't mind.
He offered the lady a bottle of Gusto but she declined. Mr Rudge went into the kitchen and grabbed a bottle for himself. He came back into the lounge and sat down on the sofa. Rudy invited the lady to plonk herself down next to him. Ivy stood and looked at the boy for a moment. She then spun around and went over to one of the cabinets. He enjoyed the view of her shapely rump as she checked out the family photos. It didn't take her long to find some snaps of Rudy as a child. "What a cutey! Is this you with mummy?" He knew which picture she was

looking at even though his view was blocked by her gorgeous body. "Yeah, that's me and the old dear. I'm ten in that shot. Literally half a life-time ago".

The man-boy supped his Gusto as he stared at the girl's splendid buttocks. "You want to go upstairs and check out my football stickers?" Ivy put the photo down and invited her host to lead the way to his "love chamber". The young fella smirked behind his hand as he rose to his feet.

Rudy sat on the edge of his bed and had a little stretch. As he went to take his shoes off Ivy sat down in his swivel chair and faced him. She flipped her little clogs off to the side and softly put her right hand on his knee. She asked "what manner of naughtiness do you get up to in here young man?" As she slowly spread her legs his mouth and eyes widened involuntarily. The student wasn't wearing any knickers. She was hairy. He was getting hard. The red head pushed herself out of the chair quite suddenly and turned away from him. "Unzip me dear". The kid did as he was told. She took her bra off once the dress was on the floor. Rudy undid his shirt as the lady tugged his trousers and pants down.

He didn't really want to draw comparisons to recent conquests as he lay there with her but he couldn't help that his brain functioned in the way that it did. She went right to the top of his league table. This Ivy was a class act. She had no trouble picking up on his masochistic tendencies. She was happy to play into them.

Just half an hour ago she had been riding him good and proper. Twenty minutes ago she had him on his knees sucking her toes. In fact she had half of her foot in his gob at one point. Ten minutes later she was giving him one of the most rigorous blow jobs of his life. He had exploded in her mouth and fallen back on his bed. He had nothing left in the tank. Now they were under the sheets together, all cuddled up.

Ivy was the talkative sort. She spoke about her friends and what they were like as people. Nicola, her taller friend, was actually a sweetheart once you got to know her. Rudy had his doubts.

She talked about her life in Lincoln. The student life. The way she spoke made him want to listen. The way she stroked his face made him want to be a part of her life.

The girl fell asleep before him. He was happy to just lay there in the dark listening to her shallow breathing.

When Rudy woke up the girl wasn't there. He reluctantly got up and had a cat like stretch. As he looked on the floor through tired eyes, searching for his pants, he saw that Ivy's clogs were right where she had kicked them off. She had not left without saying goodbye. When Rudy stepped out of his room to answer the call of nature he heard two voices downstairs. His old man was talking to Ivy. He couldn't quite make out what was being said but it sounded like a friendly exchange was taking place.

As young Mr Rudge emptied his bladder it occurred to him that his dad may well have heard the girl he was now chatting with giving him fellatio last night. The thought amused the kid.

He didn't really fancy going downstairs to make it a three way. After he had cleaned his teeth he went back into his room and sat by the window.

The man-boy looked out onto the street. Bob (Bob the Nob as Rudy called him) was cleaning his car and doing his best to ignore his wife. She kept knocking on the kitchen

window but he pretended not to hear. The lad stared down at Tawny and as he did an idea started forming.
"Tea and toast for the stud". Being called a stud was a nice little ego booster (as if he needed it). "Your daddy is lovely. We were just talking about you among other things…whatcha looking at?" She put his breakfast on the desk next to his laptop and sat down on the bed.
"How do you fancy a ride on my girlfriend?"

She wasn't as enthusiastic about the prospect of zipping about on his bike as he hoped she might have been. Even so, he was determined to win her around. She was clearly apprehensive so he had to assure her that he would be a good boy and take it nice and easy. Ivy did like the fact that he saw his bike, his steed, as a girl. "Tawny is quite the original name. Is it American?" The question invited an explanation. He told her that his Yamaha was named after Tawny Kitaen, the late actress, model and well known face in the heavy metal community back in the heyday of rock. Ivy found this to be super cute.

"I'm thinking my little blue helmet will suit you perfectly". That he could make her giggle was gratifying.

The kid kept his promise and took it nice and slow. She had never been on a bike in her life and was obviously nervous. She wrapped her arms tightly around his waist and pressed her upper chest against his back as they passed through town. Rudy decided on a whim to go south. The couple headed on down to the Gibraltar point nature reserve. Ivy did loosen her grip a little as they cruised down Gibraltar Road (but not too much).

He felt her frame relax when they stopped. The lad dismounted and took his helmet off in a showy fashion. He turned to look at her. She was making eyes at him.

"You do look sweet in that helmet Ivy". The girl smiled. "Do you have any biker leathers Rudy?" She was glad to hear that he did. "Maybe you can wear your proper riding gear next time". He was glad to hear that there was potentially a next time.

"You don't have to hold on quite so tight mate. Not that I object". Ivy digested his words and then took off her helmet. The girl exhaled. She looked to the skies and pulled herself forward on Tawny. Putting her hands on the fuel tank and redirected her gaze at Rudy she said "you're bad news I'm thinking. Am I wrong? If I took you home to meet my mother do you think she would be worried?" He suggested that she shouldn't concern herself with such questions.

A nice walk took them past a glass building

that looked like an observatory. A few old people were sat around taking in the views. The pair passed over a small bridge as they made their way towards the coast. "Maybe we should make the most of this lovely weather". Rudy moved his right hand over the girl's shapely bottom and gave her a very suggestive look. She was game. A nice big brown bush would provide sufficient cover for their outdoor romp.

Part Two: How'd you like that baby!?

Rudy suspected that his mother was keeping something from him. His suspicions had merit.
The probate process had taken months to run its course. This was to be expected. In all

that time Dora had kept a secret from her kids. Ravi had known about this from around the time of the funeral but Cyril had not been told.

Leonard had left behind quite a lot of money. He never owned his own home, nor did he have any business assets or anything like that. But he was pretty good a squirreling away cash. When Dora found out how much was due to come her way it was quite the shock. One hundred and fifty grand is no small amount of dosh.

At no point did she consider keeping it all for herself. It was always her plan to split the gift with her son and daughter. Almost all of her brother's earnings (save for a generous charitable donation) went to her. Leonard knew his sister. He knew what she would do with the money.

Ravi wondered why Dora chose not to tell Rudy and Gerry until the probate procedure was done with. He thought that this might cause problems.

When Rudy and his sister did finally find out the truth, at a special family dinner, their mother was pleased to find that the reaction was positive. Geraldine got up out of her seat to give her old dear a hug. She was delighted by this news. Immediately she knew what the money would go towards. Gerry and her partner Lisa had been wanting to get on the property ladder for a little while. This wonderful gift would allow them to put a deposit down on a seafront apartment near to where they currently lived. For the remainder of the meal her excitement grew as she imagined the reaction of her beloved Lisa. She would be over the moon. Dora loved seeing the hope and joy on her daughter's face.

She could see something in her son's eyes also. And she could hear it in his voice.

Indeed, Rudy was exhilarated. After he heard the news of his uncle's demise the lad needed to go into the garden to suck in some deep breaths. Ten minutes after he had received the news that fifty grand was coming his way fresh air was again required. As he stood looking up at the clear night sky his heart pounded. What could he do with that amount of coin? In the heat of this overwhelming moment his mind was drawing a blank.

Dora was worried about her boy. She was worried about him in a way she wasn't about her first born. She couldn't know what Rudy would do but she had her fears. This was one of the reasons why she waited a good while to drop the secret.

Ultimately Dora had to accept that her son was an adult and her brother's money was her gift to give. She couldn't predict or control the future.

When Ravi got back from his long and well planned walk he found a happy family scene. Some of the tension that Dora had been holding onto for some time had clearly evaporated. This gave him peace.

The next day over breakfast Rudy told his old man. Cyril was awash with conflicting emotions. He was happy for his son of course (while at the same time being concerned). But he was also upset with his former partner for keeping this from him. *She could have said something surely* thought he.
He was going to have to have a robust conversation with his ex-Mrs soon enough. But for now the focus was on the lad.
"Well, that's a pretty hefty wad of cash fella! Maybe you'll want to have a good think before you go splashing it around". Rudy assured him that he was thinking hard already. His gears were indeed grinding and

dreams were, even at this early stage, starting to take shape.

Around at Pez's gaff later that very day he told his best friend about the *dosh landslide* that was heading his way. Pez, despite his faults, was a good kid. He was genuinely excited for his mate and wanted him to have the time of his life.

Lee Peston knew his buddy as well as anyone did. He knew that his pal wasn't going to put the cash in a savings account. He knew that he wasn't going to look at the money and say to himself *well that's my ticket to early retirement.* No, Rudy was a young and restless spirit like himself. He had a zest for life which was at once healthy and dangerous. He would take his late uncle's money and make for himself a cracking adventure.

At work on Thursday the kid was tempted to

tell Kai about the money. He was however able to resist. If he did tell her it could spread about town via one or more of her talkative friends. If this were to happen the news might reach the ears of some more unsavory characters. Skegness had quite a few of these.

Rudy also thought about telling his boss. Was this a good idea he wondered? He was getting on well with the gaffer. In the last couple of months Clinton had come out from under his dark cloud and was clearly in a better place. Rudy had become his favourite employee as far as he could tell. He could banter with his boss. *Maybe telling him was the right thing to do.*

My Klein was pleased with the way business was going. So much so in fact that he was considering some refurbishments. He asked Rudy if he thought the place could do with *sprucing up a bit.* Mr Rudge thought that the

Plaza could do with some modernizing. The same applied to most arcades in town to be fair.

The lad appreciated that Clinton had taken the time to ask his opinion. It meant something.

A text message from Gerry got Rudy somewhat worked up. His sister told him that *mum and dad had a big slanging match about Leonard's money.* The old man had apparently gone around to Paxton Fields and given Dora both barrels. In the heat of the argument Ravi had tried to step in to defend his Mrs from the verbal barrage. Some pushing and shoving ensued. Cyril had to walk away to avoid completely losing it. Thinking back to the previous day the kid suspected that this must have happened at around lunch time. He had been in his room at about 1pm when he heard Cyril slam the front door on his way in. He could make out his dad cursing and ranting in the kitchen even though he had some music on at a fairly loud volume.

Young Mr Rudge texted his sister back. He didn't want to speak with papa just yet about any of this as he figured that he might still be pissed off. Geraldine got back to him quickly. *Mum was really upset when I talked to her on the phone last night. I hope dad comes to his senses and sees that he owes her an apology whatever his feelings might be.* Rudy agreed with his sibling. However, he could see where the old boy was coming from. He had to admit that in his shoes he might have kicked off in a similar way.

The lad wanted to hear Gerry's voice. He dialed her and she picked up on the second ring. "So when are you gonna come up to see us again?" Gerry asked. Rudy was keen to shoot up on Monday. After shifts on Saturday and Sunday he had three days off. He thought that getting out of town might help clear his excited mind. Plus the ride up to Scarborough was always enjoyable. He told her that he wouldn't be bringing his boy Pez this time as his mate would be working in the bike shop. Geraldine was glad to hear this though she didn't say as much. She found her brother's pal to be consistently irritating (she was willing to tolerate him for Rudy's sake).

Saturday at the Plaza was busy. Rudy appreciated this as it took him out of himself to a degree. There was no time for the chattering voices in his head to distract him away from his duties. When he finished at around six he headed straight home and jumped on the gorgeous Tawny. Being out and about on the bike would help him stay out of himself.

Lately he had been staying away from Lush. Pez was starting to believe that his bud might be going soft. He knew he had been sneaking off to Lincoln once every couple of weeks to see his *posh tart* Ivy. He seemed to have lost some interest in other girls from where Mr Peston was standing. Sure, he would still see Rudy knocking about with a local bird on a weekday evening, taking her for a drink and turning on the old charm. But something had changed in him since he had started his *thing* with the student. She had a hold over him in some way. Pez didn't entirely understand it but he could see those subtle changes in his mate. He didn't know half the story in truth.

In contrast to Saturday, Sunday was a slow work day. It was largely uneventful until 2.30pm when shit suddenly kicked off big time. Kai and Eric were walking the floors when Bobby Rees and his brother came barreling in. Rudy was standing at the back of the gaff talking with Clinton and watching some kids having a go at the old ten pin bowling. A nervous Eric came and told Rudy who had just arrived. Mr Rudge sighed and looked his colleague in the eye . But before he could even begin to prepare himself for the confrontation Clinton was steaming ahead. The two employees hesitated very briefly and then followed.

The pair caught up with Mr Klein just as he was upon the unwelcome visitors. Doug clocked Clinton right as he was reaching out to grab his brother from behind. One moment Bobby was staring at the fruit machine, his face a mixture of hope and anger. The next he was being swung by his leather jacket and violently launched towards the exit. The landing looked and sounded brutal. Even so, he got back to his feet real fast. The look of pure shock on his face was exquisite. The regulars were silent and stunned. Doug made a hasty retreat into the street and called for his brother to join him. There were no words from the boss. All he needed was a look. Bobby Rees got the message. Things could only get worse for him if he stayed. He snapped out of his seeming freeze and buggered off like his arse depended on it. "Well, that was exciting wasn't it kids?" Klein's words didn't really help to break the tension.

The gaffer went back to where he was standing prior to the unpleasantness. Rudy came and join him. "That was fucking awesome man" the kid exclaimed.

"Will we be seeing the little cunt again I wonder? Maybe he'll come back with his daddy". The kid let Clinton's words hang in the air for a few seconds. "I wouldn't worry about that turd. If he does put in another appearance we'll give him the business A". Klein smiled at the lad. "I'm not worried mate". He might not have been but clearly a degree of concern and unease hung over the place for the rest of the afternoon. By the evening 'the one and only' was on his trusty steed once more, feeling the power between his legs and focusing on the tarmac in front of him.

Skeggy to Scarborough was a touch over 100 miles. Rudy set off at just after 9pm. He would arrive comfortably before 11pm. Up through the Lincolnshire Wolds and up over the Humber Bridge he went. Tawny was in good form. She clearly liked the longer rides. When he arrived in town he cruised around the bay area to take it in. The yachts, the beautiful coastal houses, the stunning view of the castle; Scarborough was a class act. Rudy understood why his sister chose to move up here.

In was a windy yet clear day. When he knocked on his sister's front door he heard movement immediately. Lisa opened up. "Hiya trouble". He was almost always greeted by her in this way. "You changed your hair again?" The last time he saw her she was green. Now she was orange. "Your sister did it this time. You like?". Mr Rudge wasn't aware that his sister's talents extended to hairdressing and such. "Yeah, it suits you...makes me think of Amsterdam". She smiled at the kid's cute answer. "Gerry's just gone to the shop. She'll be back in five or ten minutes. How was the ride?" The lad gave her the A-OK sign and informed his host he was going upstairs to get out of his biker leathers and into his *street casuals.*

Gerry and Lisa had a cozy little gaff in a nice quiet street. It was alive with colour and decked out with all the creature comforts one could want. Both of the ladies liked to paint. Much of their art was displayed around the living room with some in the kitchen also. Lisa was into pottery too. One of her works, a hand crafted and over sized fruit bowl, sat on the coffee table in the lounge. Such a thing would never have been commercially produced. It wasn't perfect, but it was unique. It was one of the many human qualities to the couple's home.

The younger Mr Rudge wasn't unlike his parents in the way he took the news of Gerry having a girlfriend. It made him feel uncomfortable. He thought about how the wider community, people who knew the family but not well, might view this. Some of the reactions were sadly predictable. Many folks are lost in bigotry and rigid traditional beliefs. But he wasn't that guy. Neither was his dad. Both were able to overcome those initial negative feelings (as was Dora). This was not such a difficult thing once they got to know Lisa. Gerry had fallen in love with a wonderful woman. The family embraced Lisa as one of their own.

In came Geraldine with some milk, teabags and sugar just in time to see her brother climbing down the spiral staircase. She put the shopping down on the coffee table for a moment and greeted her kid brother with a warm hug and a smacking kiss on the cheek.

Gerry worked as a staff nurse for the N.H.S. Monday and Tuesday were generally her days off but it wasn't uncommon for her to be called in. This was a source of quiet frustration for Lisa but she understood why her partner had to keep the phone on. Lisa herself worked from home. There was no need for this administrator to be in the office anymore. The insurance company she worked for had sent many of its employees to do their jobs remotely as part of a program of cutbacks. She was glad of it. 9 to 5 was not for her.

Over a buffet style lunch Gerry talked excitedly about the prospect of the move. The ball was not yet moving but it soon would be. They would miss their current place of course. They had made some great memories here. But the money provided them with a chance to move up in the world and they were not going to pass it up.

Big sister could see that something was bothering her brother. She sensed that he perhaps wanted to talk with her in private. When Lisa went into the bedroom to check on some emails Gerry followed her in. "Would you give us a bit babe. I think a chat is in order". Lisa got it. She would keep her head down for a little while.

"You've been having a think about what to

do with your share of the dosh then Rudy mate?"

He took a small sip of his tea. Staring out of the window he cut a conflicted figure she thought.

"I'm thinking I want to get out and see the world...get out of the frog pond. I've never been any further than Holland ya know". His sister smiled from the opposite side of the table. "It's a big old world out there babe...dirty and dangerous...and beautiful. Where do you want to go?" When he said *anywhere & everywhere* Gerry rolled her eyes. "Yeah, but where first? Where's the first port of call?" The lad looked at her with a neutral expression. "There are a lot of worse ways to spend a big wad. Traveling, exploring and adventuring...would Pez be tagging along?" She got him to smile and chuckle a bit with this question. "My boy is happy where he is I reckon. If he wanted to invite himself along...". "What about your Ivy? Does she figure into your short or medium term plans?" The smile melted away, replaced by a serious expression. "I've not felt this way about a girl before. I haven't told her about the cash yet but I will". He paused to take another sip of his brew. He put the brown mug back down on the table in a very deliberate fashion. "I can't expect her to just drop what she's doing and come globe trotting with me can I? She's right in the middle of doing her dissertation. She's living the student life ya know. I can't..."

Rudy hadn't been out to watch a movie in a good while. He, Gerry and Lisa were treated to a rare gem of an Irish film about a girl who runs away from an abusive home and makes a new life for herself in London. This was not the sort of flick Mr Rudge would usually watch but he got it. He felt the emotional impact of the story.

The following day Gerry got that call Lisa was hoping she wouldn't. Someone had phoned in sick and Ms Rudge was needed to fill in. It would be a grueling 13 hour shift for her. The lad was dissapointed but he was half expecting it.

Rudy and Lisa got on very well. Of course Geraldine was mighty pleased this was the case. They had a similar sense of humour and had that good one-on-one chemistry that not everyone did. The pair spent Tuesday morning watching an assortment of funny and weird videos on WhoTube. In the afternoon the kid decided to take Tawny up the coast to Whitby. This was a 30 mile ride there and back which took in Robin Hood's Bay. The lad stopped to drink in the Bay area. It was a truly beautiful part of England. When he reached Whitby he had himself a wee walk about. The young fellow thought about the conversation he had had with big sister yesterday and how it made him feel. He knew that things were going to change real soon. He was going to step out into a wider world and experience alien places. But as he was wandering about on this breezy afternoon the past would have its say. The young fellow cast his mind back seven years to a school trip up this way. He could remember some of the bad kids in his class being punished for going off to the shops without permission, thus causing the teacher, a Mr Gregory, to do his nut and read these naughty boys the riot act.

There were two more stand out memories from his first time in this charming Yorkshire town. Young Rudy was very much taken with a girl in his set called Claire Dean. She might have been the first girl he had seen at school who had what he thought of as a grown-up hair do. She had her hair cut shorter than her female class mates and had a perm. The lad did try to chat her up on a few occasions during his Skegness Academy days but she gave him, and several other boys, the cold shoulder. She only had eyes for a dude called Malcolm Bennings who was two years older than her.

The other memory was of the the Gothic Abbey. He had heard some of his class mates say they thought it was creepy but he didn't see it in that way. He thought the site, and what was left of the building, had a magical quality to it.

On the ride back the kid full throttled it and made it back to Scarborough in no time. Tuesday evening went by fast and the following morning he was off on Tawny again. The ride helped him clear his head but the feeling didn't last long.

In his mind's eye he saw himself telling Ivy

about the money, and what he was going to do with it, in person. However, by Wednesday afternoon the kid couldn't contain himself any longer. With his mobile pressed against his ear, he waited for her to pick up. He waited and waited as he scrolled his list of favourite WhoTube videos. Just as the call was about to go to voice message the girl answered. She sounded like she was trying to catch her breath. The lad made a bit of flirty small talk as he often did. The young lady had apparently just been in a 'tedious lecture' and needed to get some caffeine in her system. Now he had her on the line some unexpected nervousness was welling up inside Mr Rudge. Even so, he was able to compose himself and say most of what he wanted to. He didn't tell her the exact amount of money he had been gifted but she could tell from the tone of the conversation that he was talking about no small chunk of change. "How'd you like that baby!?" the student almost shouted as she waited in line for coffee. She wanted to ask him questions about his uncle Leonard but felt that it was not appropriate somehow.

He was on edge. The one thing he didn't say was that he wanted her to come with him. "Where will the wind blow the young man first?" Ivy had asked. He could tell she was smiling when she said it. "I might head to California" the lad told her. He knew that in a couple of months she would be on a long break. Maybe he could ask her later if she would like to join him. If he got the timing right...

He sensed that she was excited for him.

In the months they had known each other they had not really had a crossed word. They just had a lot of fun. He still didn't know if he really *got her*. That alone could have kept the fire burning. There were layers to this girl.

That she was seeing other guys bothered him not one bit. She was young and hungry as he was. What mattered was their connection. They talked on the phone for half an hour. He arranged to come and see her sometime next week. Perhaps it would be the last time he saw her in a while.

As he walked to work on Thursday the nervous and unwelcome feeling was with him once more. He got to the Plaza twenty minutes early and told Clinton, who seemed to be in a good mood, that he needed a private chat with him. Mr Klein could see from the look on his employee's face that this might not be a lighthearted affair. His assumption was that Rudy was simply moving on to a different job. The bloke and the man-boy sat down in Clinton's wee office. Rudy knew that his boss tried to cram too much stuff into this small space. When he sat down in the box shaped room, on the opposite side of the desk to Mr Klein, the clutter felt oppressive. "So what's the story buddy? Did the Yamaha shop make you an offer you couldn't refuse?" The boss's easy smile put the kid at ease. As he began to explain his situation the kid was taken aback somewhat by how interested Clinton appeared to be. He would be surprised further by the gaffer's response. "Mate, I had an uncle who left me some money...many years ago. I wouldn't have been too much older than you actually. You know what I did? I invested it in my first business endeavour. The whole thing went tits up in six months. My man, if I had my time again I would probably go traveling like yourself". Rudy resisted the urge to ask what the endeavour in question involved. It may well have been dodgy.

The boss asked where he was heading to. As

he had told Ivy just yesterday Rudy said he was California bound. "I thought I might go to Hollywood and have a nosy around". Klein let out a wee chuckle. "You should be careful down there buddy. Plenty of shady cunts in the City of Angels. Big homeless population too. At least there was the last time I went. That would have been more than ten years ago mind". Rudy was aware of Los Angeles's bad reputation. The horror stories he had heard did not put him off wanting to see the place with his own eyes.

"You will be missed my friend. I might find it tricky to replace you". The young fella appreciated his boss's kind words. "When you get back from your adventures come in and tell me a tale or two A". Of course Rudy said he would. He gave the gaffer two weeks notice and he asked him not to tell Kai or Eric about the money. Clinton agreed to keep it under his hat. Young Mr Rudge would tell his colleagues later that he was simply leaving to 'have some personal time and space away from the workaday world'. Kai suspected that he was up to something but she wasn't willing to press him. Perhaps she would miss him just a little even if she wouldn't say as much.

The next week flashed by. 'The one and only' had found himself a cheap plane ticket as well as a budget hotel. It was a Sunday morning when he confirmed these purchases. The trip was on and his excitement naturally grew.

He and Cyril had a long father and son chat that afternoon at the kitchen table. His dad was not shy about giving his boy the advice he thought he needed to hear. Rudy believed he was taking in his dad's words but the old man could see that his boy was not being as receptive as he would have liked. Looking his

son in the eye he could see that the youngster was already on his way.
Sunday evening saw the lad around at Paxton Fields having a meal with his mum and Ravi. Dora was not quite as forthcoming with the parental advice as was Cyril but she was full of anxiety. Of course her son picked up on this as he tucked into the old beef roast. He assured her that he was more than capable of 'fending for himself'. He thought himself street wise and *tuned in to the game*. Ravi warned him about the latest scams that con-men were perpetrating (according to what he was reading online and in the papers). Rudy said that he had heard variations of what his mum's fella was on about. But Dora was not so worried about the possibility of Rudy getting scammed out of some change or anything similar. She was worried about his well-being, physical, emotional and mental. She was concerned he

would lose himself on the journey.

"Call me as soon as you're settled in L.A. You know I'm nosy sweetheart. I want to know what you're up to". This is what the old dear told him while he was helping her with the washing up. Her words would stick with him. She wasn't actually a nosy parker. She just needed to know he was safe. She wanted to listen to his voice and *hear* how he was doing.

He could get off when she didn't do it. He could still do vanilla. But everything was so much better, so much more intense when she did it.

She could just about get her small hands around his throat. She would start off nice and slow, teasing him with her soft feminine fingers. As the ride sped up and she really built up steam the grip would tighten. Today, with the big pay off drawing close she rode him with near ferocity as her two thumbs pushed down just above his Adam's apple. She could make him crazy for real in moments like this one. As he climaxed he was truly out of his mind. This lustful abandon was so dangerous.

She had grown to love his darkness. Sprawled out naked on the bed together he did his best to put into words the thoughts that danced behind his hazel eyes. "So, I guess you have some plans for when you break up for the summer? You'll be going to see your folks and what not?" It was obvious what he was hoping to hear. "Yes, back to Sussex I will be heading my dear...for a couple of weeks I would imagine. Then, who knows". She gave her lover one of those looks. She jumped up off the bed and was behind her bathroom door in a flash, leaving the kid to stretch out. He stared at his flaccid member as he listened to the girl singing a

Cher number from back in the day.

A whirlwind of goodbyes had led him to this. Pez had taken the day off work to come down to Heathrow and see his friend away. On the train they had drank a couple of cans of lager while bantering loudly. An older couple had complained about their rowdiness and a stern looking ticket inspector had told them off. This amused Mr Peston more than it did Rudy. The excitable youth was thinking of kicking off but his mate talked him into a better head space.

Neither of them had set foot inside Heathrow before. The lads were impressed by the scale and buzz of the place. Feeling a wee bit tipsy the pair decided to do some 'bird watching' as they sat in the self-service all day breakfast restaurant on the first floor. A trio of Spanish ladies caught Pez's eye. Mr Rudge was taken by the blonde of the group. She had a round owl like face with kind chocolate brown eyes. Her gentle laughter was endearing. As he was stealing glances at the girl his friend whispered in his left ear. "You'll be knee deep in California pussy by this time tomorrow pal". The heat from Pez's mouth made Rudy wince. He turned to his buddy and gave a familiar smirk. But as he looked down at what was left of his greasy fry-up a more serious expression formed.

"I'm going to miss…Tawny. Getting out on the bike…Going riding with you".

Always being the guy who wanted to lift his best mate's spirits Lee responded. "When you swing back this way lad Tawny will be sat there waiting for you. We can ride wherever you want. Somewhere we've never been maybe A".

Rudy was about to go somewhere he'd never been. He was about to travel thousands of miles across a vast ocean and all the way across the North American continent. This would only be his third time on a plane. He was nervous about the long ride and how he would handle it.

Rudy checked himself and his big black suitcase in. Then it was time to say farewell to his partner in crime. He could see the sadness in Lee's face. "Go have it large yer bellend" said the lad, giving his pal a playful punch on the shoulder. Rudy's hopeful broad smile broke Pez a little inside. He stood fixed to the spot as Mr Rudge walked away at pace.

Off went the kid to get molested by security. Once he'd made it past that annoying obstacle and walked through the duty free area it was time to grab a fat wad of US dollars from the exchange. He showed his passport to the friendly middle aged lady in the booth and waited as she counted out his money.

Finally getting that American green in his hand was a tremendously exciting moment. He spent a good couple of minute just looking at it as he stood off to the side of the exchange. Eventually he stuffed it into a plastic sleeve and popping it into his carry bag.

He amused himself for a little while in the retro arcade next to the pub/restaurant. Playing on the old first person shooter game ate up some time. Once he had exhausted his change he went next door and indulged in a pre-flight pint. That cold glass of ale tasted as good as any he had ever had. He downed it in five minutes flat.

Mr Rudge was at his departure gate a good half an hour prior to boarding calls. There would be quite the crowd on this flight.

There were quite a few families and young people in groups.
When they called forward those in business class only a handful of well dressed lone travelers stepped forward.
The excitement grew and grew. He gazed at the large British Airways Airbus on the tarmac shining in the sun. Despite its impressive size something told him it couldn't possibly fit all these people on in.
He stepped forward and handed his passport and boarding card to the flight attendant. The beautiful young lady waved him through. As he stepped through the door of the plane he once again presented his pass and was directed down towards row 33.
This was a direct flight. He would be in the air for half a day.
Rudy Rudge shoved his cabin bag into the compartment above and shuffled into his window seat. He set his carry bag down

between his legs and took off his coat. A young couple came and sat in the seats next to him. They spoke softly in a European language he didn't recognize.

After a series of announcements the airbus crawled out to its spot on the runway. The kid looked around at the people as they fiddled with headphones and stared at the screens in front of them. One guy looked like he was ready for bed already.

The plane roared forward. The take off was an intense experience for the kid. He got a real buzz out of it.

During the assent the lad looked down at London. So many busy folks going about their lives. The grass did somehow seem greener from up here. Passing through the clouds as they continued to rise, Rudy suddenly found himself thinking of Leonard. He closed his eyes and tried to visualize the last time he saw his uncle. As he did this his mother entered his mind. Then he was pulled in the direction of thinking about the last meal he had had with her and Ravi.

The young man was able to lose himself in some music for a while. Even so, his mind just kept on racing. He would not sleep on this flight.

The first 24 hours did not go smoothly. The plane was stuck on the tarmac at LAX for more than an hour. By the time they got to the gate everyone was agitated to some degree.

Rudy was tired and wired. He got his suitcase from baggage reclaim and was eager to be on his way.

The hustle and bustle in the arrival area was a sight to behold. He was finally here in an alien land!

He managed to find the free shuttle service to the train station and from there he took the green line into the city center. He thought that he had a good idea where the hotel was. He had the directions written down on a little piece of paper he had tucked into his passport. He was able to find the street with relative ease but the number of the place didn't appear to exist.

It was just after midday. This level of heat the lad had not felt before.

Rudy asked at a local seven eleven if they knew where the hotel was. The store clerk, who Rudy thought looked like Tupac, had no idea. He then asked a random man on the street but he was non the wiser. At this point he thought it best to give the hotel a call on the number they had provided. He was met with a voice mail service and he felt the anxiety and frustration creeping in.

What could he do next? Did this place even exist he began to wonder. Becoming thirsty he decided to go into another store. He grabbed himself a soft drink and then found a shaded spot next to a cake shop. He sat on his suitcase (which he was getting tired of dragging around) and tried to gain some composure as he gulped down the cold beverage.

He looked around and saw several other hotels on the street. They all looked fairly run down. He saw a few homeless folks camped outside the liquor store. A couple of them were looking his way.

The kid thought it might be a good idea to go into one of the hotels and ask if they knew where his accommodation was. He gave the phone number another go first. Again it went to voice mail. And so he walked across the street and entered the Dayton Hotel. The receptionist's desk and office area were fenced off from everything else. The set up looked hostile rather than welcoming.

Rudy approached the desk and politely asked

the lady if she knew where the Jacobs Hotel was. He handed her his scribblings. The lady smiled as she looked over the details he'd wrote through her thick rim glasses. "You're from England huh?" The kid nodded and answered in the affirmative. "You see that side street next to the seven eleven out there?" She pointed out of the front door and Rudy turned to follow the direction of her finger. "You need to go down there and walk up to the end of the block. Your place will be on the right hand side. They have the sign above the door in big blue letters".

The young fella breathed a sigh of relief. He had found his home for the next fortnight. This was a self-check in establishment. In the email they had sent him it had been explained that it was a door code system (no keys). He entered the first four digit code on the heavy metal door. He smiled broadly as it unlocked with a squeak and a click. He went up the stairs to the second door, lifting his suitcase with all his strength. This black gated security door looked like something he'd seen in movies set in New York. He entered the second code. Again success. The sound of his entrance must have gotten a few people's attention as he heard movement in a couple of the rooms. The walls were dirty in the corridor and the orange paint was peeling off around the top. There was a musky smell in the air. He didn't smell too good himself at this point. Following the numbers he marched towards room 17. The code for the second security door was supposed to be the same code to open his room. But he found that his room was open... In he went to find a space a wee bit smaller than his bedroom back in Skeggy. The bed sheets were the first thing that caught his attention. They looked very psychedelic. He had a small fridge which he was happy about. On top of the fridge there was a microwave with a crack on the screen. He had a dirty looking sink above which sat a dirty looking mirror. He checked the tap and was glad to find he had running water. There was no cupboard or cabinets. There was a desk with one draw, and there was a metal bar running from one side of the room to the other. A stack of coat hangers were on the floor in one corner.

Rudy unloaded his clothes, his documents and his electronic equipment. Sorting it all out was not as much work as he thought it might be. He managed to get everything where he wanted it to be in roughly twenty minutes.
When he was done he went out the door and looked for the shower. It didn't take much searching. It was right next to his room.

Being confronted by a stinking laundry bin in the bathroom and a soiled floor area was obvious not what he wanted. He grabbed a towel off the rail, stripped down, and got in the shower.

It felt so fucking good under the warm jet of water. He rubbed the blue shower gel he found on the window ledge all over his body and groaned loudly in pleasure. He didn't care who heard.

Back in his room he lay on his bed and took in the place. He had a clock on the wall which looked like the ones they had at school. It being almost 1pm made him think of lunchtime mischief at the Academy all those years ago.

He had felt it come on him like a drug. He was being hit by a wave of tiredness he couldn't resist.

The 'one and only' woke up suddenly. There

was some sort of argument going on right outside. A couple of what sounded like younger men were loudly going at each other. Rudy's brain couldn't quite process what was going on. He heard a door slam and the voices became muffled. This was not a great way to be woken up.

The lad turned on the bedside lamp and looked at the clock through squinted eyes. He saw that it was almost 9pm. He had been out of it for 8 hours! He sat up and rubbed his eyes. As the lad came to his senses and stood to have a stretch the angry voices stopped. The kid was hungry. Not in a peckish way. His guts were doing some serious complaining. He grabbed his wallet and jacket and made for the door. As Rudy walked towards the end of the corridor he noticed that one guest had his door wide open. He glanced in as he passed and glimpsed a man, unconscious on the floor, next to what might have been a

water bong.
Stepping out onto the street he was met with maybe twice as many homeless folks as had been around in the daylight. Less than two metres from Jacobs front door was a rough looking lady smoking on a glass pipe. The man sat next to her rubbed a piece of tinfoil between his fingers as he stared at Rudy. The kid walked swiftly and a little nervously towards the store he had been in this afternoon. However, he found that it had closed a couple of hours ago. The only place still open was the liquor store.
Young Mr Rudge waited for a taxi cab and a couple of kids on electric scooters to pass him. He crossed the street with a degree of apprehension. He was relieved that none of the homeless people seemed to pay any mind to him as he went through them near to the entrance.
The lad got himself a couple of cans of

SudWeiser, a large bag of potato chips and a few protein chocolate bars. The boy from Skegness waited in line behind one guy telling a story about what he had seen a cop do to a woman he knew earlier in the day. His tale appeared to wind the clerk up a fair bit. Rudy just wanted to pay for his shit and get back to his room.

Back behind the second security door, he felt safe enough. The unconscious man's door was still open. This time as he passed someone came out to meet him. A wee ginger cat rubbed against his leg and meowed for attention. A smiling Rudy bent down to pet the cute animal. He gave the fur ball some chin stretches which were well received and appreciated.

4 weeks later: Text messages between Rudy & Pez.

Saturday 15.13 GMT

Rudy: How's it going you big handsome bastard? It's just after 7 in the morning here. Haven't been to bed yet lol. Still pissed :D

15.41 GMT
Pez: Hey bezzy :) I was wondering when you'd check in. How's life in the California sunshine my man?

15.47 GMT
Rudy: Fuck me mate. It's a different world out here. This city is a hot mess. Plenty of fuckin' headbangers around as you can imagine.
Yesterday was my first time on Long Beach. Some of the houses man...how the other half lives.

15.55 GMT
Pez: So, little bit different from Grand Parade then? x) I bet the houses aren't the only thing young Rudy was looking at down at the beach A?

16.01 GMT
Rudy: There is a God Mr Peston...and he is good.

16.02 GMT
Pez: hahahaha. So where is your go to massage parlour? Are you in the middle of the action zone?

16.05 GMT
Rudy: No parlours man. Found myself an escort. Seen her a few times now. The arse on her. You would die bro. You would fucking die.

16.06 GMT
Pez: More details mofo!

16.09 GMT
Rudy: Laters my good man. I'll give you the *juicy* later. You looking after my bike kid?

16.11 GMT

Pez: And he's asking about Tawny x) Took you long enough. She's fine dickhead. Took her out to Boston just yesterday. Almost crashed a couple of times as I always do ;)

16.15 GMT
Rudy: I'll open you up like a tin of beans boy! :D
I'm going to bed anyway. Speak to you later bellend.

16.18 GMT
Pez: Don't be a stranger kid. Stay classy spunk bubble ;)

When he finally did get around to calling his mum and letting her hear his voice he had been in California for more than a month. Dora was quite upset with her boy. She told him that she had been getting worried. His careless and dismissive attitude only upset her more. He suggested that he was going to hang up if she kept "giving him aggro". Dora wanted to give the arrogant wee shit a piece of her mind. But she didn't. She composed herself and asked in a curious tone what the lad had been getting up to. His answers were more guarded than she expected. Ravi was giving her concerned looks from across the living room.

The middle aged woman ended up keeping him on the phone for 30 minutes, talking about all the latest Skeggy gossip. She wasn't boring him. He was happy to hear that life on the Lincolnshire coast carried on in his absence. Rudy hung up quite suddenly. Dora sent him a text asking him to call her in a few days. He sent a love heart emoji straight back.

Rudy was telling the truth when he told Pez that he'd found an escort with *an arse on her.* But her bottom wasn't by any means the most impressive thing about this lady.

Her real name was Dana Maddows. She may have been known to those who followed *indie wrestling* as *Athena*. She stood at an impressive 6 foot 2 inches and had an amazing muscular physique. Unfortunately due to prescription drug abuse and a host of legal problems she had lost most of her life time earnings from the wrestling business and now worked as a *high class escort* in and around L.A.

Dana had no problems being able to lift or carry or do anything she pleased with most normal sized guys. Rudy Rudge was a normal sized guy.

During his first few sessions the kid wanted the lift and carry experience. He wanted her to put him in a number of classic wrestling holds; holds which gave him more than a taste of how strong she actually was.

On a sunny Monday afternoon the lad walked into her place feeling refreshed after a long sleep. He greeted Dana with a single red rose and a box of chocolates. Some women might have seen this approach as corny but not Ms Maddows. She found Rudy to be a cutie pie.

Unlike his previous sessions he had texted her the day before to lay out what he wanted her to do to him. She appreciated his kinky imagination.

Dana would work, on request, with a woman named Becky. This Becky was claiming to be twenty four but the lad thought she might be more than thirty years old based on her pics. Dana gave her age as thirty eight.

Becky was to act as the referee and the photographer. The man boy would wear the mint green wrestling attire his host provided. He wore it with a horny delight.

The *match* wouldn't go long. Dana, *Athena*, overpowered the lad with a clothesline followed by a body-slam on her navy blue gym mat. She then delivered a big leg drop and got the three count. Her hand was raised in victory as she placed her foot on the chest of her conquered foe. She would then pose with the kid in various shots. Becky was enjoying herself as was Dana. So was the client which was of course the all important factor.

In one photo Rudy was sat down in an upright position, leaning against Dana's leg as she held him by the hair. His wrestling tights had been pulled down around his ankles. In another shot the lucky young fellow was in a head scissors move, his bare arse in the air. He had to pay only a small amount extra to have the photos sent to his phone.

He walked out of Dana's gaff feeling like a million dollars. As far as he was concerned this counted as therapy.

Several occurrences in quick succession led him to the conclusion that it was time to move on.

The first happening took place in the small hours of a Tuesday morning. One of the hotel guests came banging on his door and others too. The guy was shouting and screaming about the arrival of *enemy troops* and was trying to order people out into the street as if he was a military commander or something. Rudy thought that he might be having some kind of psychotic break. He wouldn't have opened his door for love or money. Eventually, after 20 minutes of insane shouting, the cops came to take the man away. He did not go quietly. After everything had calmed down the kid found he had plenty of sympathy for the disturbed and disturbing man.

On the Thursday Mr Rudge was witness to a convenience store robbery. A young dude with very intense blue eyes wearing a dark green jacket pulled out a black pistol and stuck it in the cashier's face. He spoke in an almost whisper as he told the shaken employee to open the register. Quite rightly he put up no resistance. Rudy was stood near to the soft drink fridge, only about ten feet away from the terrifying scene. The lad's heart was pounding something fierce as the criminal left the store in a hurry. An old fellow who had been stood in one of the aisle ways came and offered some comfort to the cashier. Rudy was impressed that this store clerk, who couldn't have been any older than he was, managed to keep it together and call the cops on his cell phone. He said to the police that he knew the robber by face and name. When Mr Rudge stepped up to pay for his drink the interaction seemed surreal. "That was crazy" said the Skegness native. That was all he could offer.

As the day progressed the kid found that he had been deeply affected by what he had seen. He didn't sleep much that night. But it was perhaps the last thing that occurred, on the Saturday, which scared him the most. As he was crossing the street near to a cinema a man he was walking behind turned to him and said (while looking him straight in the eye) "I don't believe in peace and good will fun boy. I don't believe in live and let live...that's why I carry a piece, you feel me". Rudy Rudge did the right thing. He side stepped the individual and avoided eye contact. As he moved away an animal fear gripped the kid. *Am I going to be shot?* He felt it possible.

He stepped into the cinema and headed to the restroom. He was sweating as he sat down in the cubicle.

The kid checked out of his hotel two days earlier than he had been due to leave. He headed to the airport, having arranged a short flight to Vegas the previous evening. He wasn't in the best of moods when he arrived in Nevada. But he soon found the neon surroundings gave him a positive bounce. He checked himself into a gaff called Super 88 on the North Strip.

Part Three: Cursed Coin

Mr Rudge was back in Skegness. New York was still fresh in his mind.
Coming back into England via Heathrow, Rudy met his buddy Pez in almost the exact place where they had parted ways just two months ago. Lee was surprised that his pal wasted no time in reaching out to give him a hug. His friend didn't smell so good.
On the train back up to Lincolnshire young Mr Peston was hoping for stories of

debauchery. But his mate was somewhat subdued. Perhaps it was just jet lag and fatigue thought he.

Rudy had taken to wearing a sheep skin jacket and a very worn pair of chewing gum white jeans. He had picked these items up in a thrift store in Queens. Lee thought they made him look like a bit of a scrubber but he didn't pass comment.

When Rudy got back to North Parade he of course wanted to stand outside his house and admire Tawny. Absence had made his heart grow fonder. She looked even more beautiful than usual in the afternoon summer sun. Cyril spotted him and came out to greet his boy. He hugged the young buck tightly with a tear in his eye. "How have you been fella?" the old man softly asked. For some reason Rudy found that he couldn't muster up an answer.

Cyril was in truth a little bit pissed off with his

son. The kid had only called him once while on his travels. It's not like he was expecting a call everyday. But he did think the boy who he brought up might be more inclined to keep him in the loop. He didn't want to show the lad his discontent.

The man-boy's mother and sister too were kind of upset with him for the same basic reason as Cyril. Rudy had texted Gerry twice during his nine weeks in America. These had been vague messages about what he'd done the day prior.

The last message had been more than three weeks ago.

Gerry knew through her mother that Rudy was coming home for a bit. She had a mind to come down from Scarborough on the Monday and maybe give him a piece of her mind after she had hugged and kissed the idiot.

On Saturday evening Cyril and the lad would go over to Paxton Fields. It was to be a meal and a few drinks with Dora and Ravi.

His mum had an emotional reaction to seeing her boy coming in through the door behind his dad.

To see his mum start crying right in front of him gave the lad that unpleasant feeling in the pit of his stomach. He moved to comfort her which in itself made the lady jump. Ravi managed to break the tension by talking some bollocks. He guided the little group into the living room where snacks and drinks awaited.

Rudy hadn't sat down to have a hot meal since he left for the U.S. This was something that he missed. Fish & Chips with mushy peas and curry was a lovely treat. Even his dad and Ravi bickering with each other couldn't spoil his good vibes. 'The one and only' washed down the food with a cold can of lager as the family crashed out in front of the wide screen.

It was not just the home cooked meal that the kid had been missing. It took him till this moment to realized it. He was stealing glances at his parents as they watched their favourite crappy old sitcom. They were contented and happy like this. This was their element. Things were familiar here. Familiar and safe. This town was familiar and safe. This town was his home. It was a part of his being.

By midnight his old man had gone home and his old dear had gone to bed. Left to watch the late night football highlights were just he and Ravi. And here they were laughing and bantering. This was not something that had occurred in the past. Ravi was the only one who had complimented the kid on his new choice of clothing.

"I kind of envy what you've been doing ya know. I wish I'd gotten out there, to America I mean...wish I'd seen a little more of the big wide world". Rudy wanted him to go on but he appeared to clam up after he had said this.

Maybe Ravi was better off for the things he hadn't seen.

Young Mr Rudge was in a place he didn't want his family knowing about. Vegas had taken its toll and New York was even worse. *Be careful what you wish for.* An old cliche yes, but one which was hitting home for the son of Cyril and Dora.

In Nevada he had hooked up with a young black woman who said she was from Austin. He figured that she might have been homeless judging by her dress and sketchy behaviour.

She really appreciated that he was willing to let her stay at his place on the North Strip. He brought her food and alcohol, and he told her she could 'hang out' with him as long as he was in the city. Of course she knew that this British boy would want something in return.

Sleeping at his mum's that night he got not a wink of sleep. He was in a thought loop that he couldn't break. The last night he had been at the Super 88 he had come as close as he ever had to *checking out.* The girl, Deja, choked him unconscious with her belt while they were fucking on the toilet. She thought she had actually killed him for one awful moment.

Rudy came around on the bathroom floor. Deja had put him in the recovery position. He had pulled himself against the bathtub as he regained his vision and hearing. The girl

put her clothes on and left soon after this horror show had played out.
He must have leaned against that bathtub, naked and cold, for almost an hour as he stared into the abyss.
This dark thought loop wouldn't let him have peace.

It would have been just before 7.30am on Sunday when he got back on Tawny for the first time in a long time. He had actually dreamt of this. In his dream he was in his leathers and he had Ivy on the back, her arms around his waist.
Now the moment was here. He did not need his biker gear. He did not need Ivy either.
He put his helmet on, kick started her up and went tearing down North Parade without an idea where he was going.
Given that he hadn't actually slept since he was on the plane coming back this ride was

not a wise move. Further, his emotional state was such that focus was lacking. On top of this simply being on the bike again was intoxicating.

He was not even aware if he was headed north, south or west. It did not matter.

He was riding to escape the past. He was hoping to shut his thoughts away and insert himself into the present 100%. Rudy was able to achieve this.

This was the day that he would be made to pay a price for his risk taking.

All he saw was the other side of the busy junction. He didn't see the small blue Nissan as it slammed into Tawny. The kid was folded off of the windscreen and the bike was sent bouncing & skidding off to the side of the road. The young woman in the vehicle feared she must have killed the lad. Many of the motorists around her too thought they must have just witnessed a fatality. But to the amazement of onlookers the young biker got back to his feet and was able to cast his gaze upon his fallen steed. He had not even registered the nasty cuts he had on both arms or the scrape on his left leg.

The lady in the Nissan was in shock. She tried to get a grip and think about what she was going to do next but nothing would come. Fortunately a couple of motorists who had stopped at the sight of the accident had already called the police and the ambulance. One fellow who had put a call in cautiously moved towards Rudy. As he got closer the young man removed his helmet and looked the bloke in the eye. The older man didn't like what he saw. The kid looked angry and confused. "What the fuck happened?!" Mr Rudge demanded to know. "Don't worry bud. Paramedics are on the way". The man's words were met with a hostile glare.

The kid had been completely uncooperative with the first responders. On arrival at the hospital he took on an aggressive tone with the staff. However, after a strong pain killer had been administered he did calm down and go inside himself.

He spent the next couple of hours going over what had happened. In his mind he was not at fault for the crash. The bitch that hit him was. He would find out later that the investigating police would have a different take on who was to blame for the accident. It was not until the next day, almost 24 hours after the smash up, that Rudy called his old man and told him where he was and what had gone down. Cyril was quick to come to the side of his son. He was nervous as hell when he walked into the hospital (like many people he hated them) but he breathed a mighty sigh of relief when he saw that his

boy appeared to be in good health. He thought it best not to call Dora right away when Rudy told him that he would probably get released tomorrow. No point worrying his former partner thought Cyril.
The lad did indeed get cleared to go home the following day.

He was happy to be back in his room but that happiness would soon evaporate. He would learn that Tawny was a write off. His beloved steed had been damaged beyond repair. In the hospital he had convinced himself that it wasn't that bad. He had looked at her by the side of the road. She wasn't a mangled heap by any stretch. *But they're telling me she's a goner?* The young fellow was proper gutted. More bad news and bad vibes were to follow. As he recovered in his bedroom he had his mum and his sister in his ear giving him the business. Gerry really let him have it.

He wasn't inclined to argue.

A week after the incident he would find out that the police were passing the file of his case to the Crown Prosecution Service. This news might have worried a person who was thinking reasonably.

Of course Pez came round to see him everyday during his recuperation and he did his best to cheer his mate up (with limited success). Rudy told him that he wanted to get back out there on the road "to prove himself" as soon as possible. Lee was certain that if his buddy asked to borrow his bike for a spin he would have to say no. He was glad that 'the one and only' didn't ask.

Rudy surprised himself by how pleased he was to see Kai and Eric's faces as he rolled into the Plaza to say hi. Kai asked some vague questions, trying to get an idea what dirty shit he had been up to this past couple

of months. Mr Rudge held his tongue and played it coy.
When he asked if Clinton was about Eric did a face drop and Kai's eyes widened as she inhaled.
Rudy could tell that she had a story to tell. She invited Mr Rudge to sit down with her on a couple of stools round the back of a currently broken fruit machine. Kai spoke in a hushed tone as she explained what had happened. Rudy wasn't massively surprised by what he heard.
Bobby Rees had clearly been humiliated on that day when Clinton had thrown him like a rag doll and sent him packing. The ordeal must have been too much for wee Bob to bear. Klein had wondered out loud if the boy might get his father involved. As it turned out he would. Rees senior (Jake) came into the place on a Sunday afternoon armed with a metal pipe, eyes blood shot angry,

demanding to know where Clinton was 'hiding'. The boss heard the loud threatening voice from his little office.

In reality Klein was not the sort of guy to hide from trouble. He came out to meet his man with a rounders bat (that he kept in the draw of his desk). When Jake saw Clinton holding his tool he began to shake with rage. Klein confidently sized his enemy up.

Jake took a swing. It would be the only swing he would take. Clinton dodged the blow and delivered a cracking back handed shot across the top of Jake's skull. The impact was heard by all three of the regular customers as well as Kai who was stood a good twenty feet away. It didn't quite knock the man out but it did very much incapacitate him.

"So I'm stood there calling the cops with everyone else standing there in like shock and amazement. Then, as I'm waiting, phone ringing, Clinton kicks the twat in the face. I honestly thought he'd killed him".

The police showed up and tried to establish what had gone on. Jake was taken to hospital. Fortunately for him and Klein it turned out that he wasn't badly hurt. Clinton was arrested and later released. Every witness stood up for the owner. Even so, the stress of the whole thing had led Klein to a dark place and he decided that a vacation was in order. Three weeks ago he had gone over to Amsterdam. He didn't say when he would be returning. Now it was one of Klein's old mates, Victor Brice, running the gaff and looking after the office. Rudy had only ever met Victor in passing a couple of times. He seemed like an old school tough guy.

Young Mr Rudge was intrigued by what he had heard. He still had Clinton's phone number and had a mind to give him a call at some point. Maybe they could have an interesting conversation.

Taking the train over to Lincoln was a different experience. It gave him more time to think which wasn't necessarily a good thing in a situation like this.

He had only texted her a few times during his time overseas. Although she was clearly curious he didn't give her much to go on. She got the feeling he was too busy or immersed in whatever he was doing to pay her much in the way of attention. But now he was on his way over to her place. She had texted him the day prior, extending the invitation.
She invited him over because she genuinely liked the kid. She felt he deserved a face to face to let him know *what was up.* In a couple of days time she would head back to her parents.
When he showed up at her door she got the distinct impression that he was expecting

something (something like a sweaty and hard welcome home). He was to be dissapointed. In the time Rudy had been living the *high life & low life* in America Ivy had hooked up with a guy called Robin from her English Literature class. It had been a slow burner between these two (nothing like the red hot relationship she had had with young Mr Rudge). They had started out as friends and grown closer over time until romance finally blossomed. She felt as if this thing had a good chance of lasting. She was looking forward to introducing him to her folks soon. She had not been looking forward to the spot she currently found herself in. Here she was giving a young man the gentle let down. She could see him deflating before her eyes. It was not a pleasant thing to have to do but she felt it was better not to lead the lad on. Even though he was hurting Rudy attempted to put a brave face on it. He hung around for a while and even told Ivy a tale or two about his time in L.A and Vegas.

Ivy cared about him. She cared enough to be concerned for his well-being. When he told her about Tawny and the accident he could see that he pulled at her heart strings. "I don't want to sound like your mum babe but you've got to be more careful out there". He sort of glazed over as she continued to offer words of caution.

"So what will you do next? Is the young man going to head back out there into the unknown?" He had a good idea what his next move was going to be but he did not feel like sharing it with the lady.

He wanted to make a graceful exit. He wished her and Robin all the best and told her (in all seriousness) that if things didn't work out she could give him a bell. He could tell that this pissed her off a little bit which he was pleased with.

He took one last look at her place as he walked down the street. When one is wounded in moments like this the last thing you want to see is a happy couple coming towards you, smiling broadly and holding hands. As they passed he spat loudly and aggressively on the pavement.

Rudy was glad to hear that the Crown Prosecution Service would not be proceeding with a case against him. Naturally he was kicked into a good mood for the day upon getting the news. He and Pez would hit Lush later on with the intent of getting fucked up and chasing the tail.

This was a Wednesday night so Custer's wasn't as packed as it might have been on the weekend. In fact it was a slow night. The two lads sat at the bar going hard and heavy, pint after pint. After the forth Pez got the feeling he might want to slow down a little. Rudy had no such feeling.

At around 8pm a group of woman came into the bar area and started whooping it up. The two lads watched on and tried in vein to figure out what the deal was. In the end they decided it must be a hen party.

"How fairs it ladies? Can I...may I have the pleasure of buying you all a round of drinks?" Mr Rudge wasn't so sure on his feet as he thought he might have been when he came over to make his generous offer. Of course the girls were happy to take him up on this. The smaller blonde from the gang went up to the bar and did the honours. Rudy waved at the barman and pointed at himself. He then searched for Pez with his blurry vision but couldn't pick him out. As if by magic his mate appeared behind him. He introduced himself as Charles Halsey to the tall mousy haired lady in the silk grey outfit. Rudy had to have a good long look at these girls in his inebriated state before deciding that they weren't local. On the fly he took a fancy to playing silly buggers like his pal. Tonight he was going to be Thomas Kensworth. He liked the way it sounded when he said it out loud to the other blonde in the pack. She wasn't quite as taken with it as he was. Nevertheless, he persisted with what he believed to be a handy charm offensive. Delusionally, he thought he was in with a solid chance. His mate by contrast was able to read the room. By the time six of the Skegness F.C lads came strolling into the gaff Pez was doing his best to gently move Rudy out of Custer's. "Let's go get a bit of air lad, then we'll jump on the dance floor in a bit A". Rudy couldn't get why Lee wanted to go. *The birds just needed to loosen up a bit. They just needed a wee be more liquid persuasion.*

The girl that 'the one and only' was coming on strong with had had enough of his touching and leering. She put a hand up in his face and turned away, giving her full attention to one of her friends. The young drunken fellow did not take kindly to this. He proceeded to 'accidentally' knock her drink over. "Oh, I am sorry sweetheart. Silly me. I'll get you another". Everyone in the girls group got the feeling it was time to walk away. They tried to make a quick dash towards the exit but Rudy cut them off. "Was it something I said ma dears?" One of the blondes was quick to fire back. "Mate, take the fucking hint. And maybe go home and sleep it off".

Good friend that he was, Mr Peston once again tried to reason with his pal and get him outside for a breather. But Rudy wasn't having it. "What a bunch of stuck up little cunts...try and be nice and this is how it fucking goes A". Lee could see it coming but there wasn't anything he could do at this point. Two of the Skegness F.C lads came over and asked if the ladies needed any help. Before any of them could respond the angry and frustrated kid told the 'white knights' to go and sit back down. "This is just a little misunderstanding boys. Go back to your drinks A". The larger chap, a center back for his club, didn't like Rudy's attitude at all. He could see that the guy in front of him was embarrassed and spoiling for a fight. But he wasn't looking to escalate. He looked to Pez. Leaning in, he whispered some well meaning advice in Lee's ear. The footballers then went to sit back down at their table and the girls again attempted to leave. Once more Rudy started mouthing off. From behind Pez wrapped his arms around his mate's waist and lifted him off of the ground. He carried him back to their spot at the bar and said to the dude running the show "we're ready to settle the bill". This got a laugh from a couple of the girls as they blew out of the door. The footballers looked on with a degree of concern.

The drunken man-boy appeared to sober up for just a moment. He took out a wad of notes and fingered through them. He paid the barman and told him to keep the change. Then, in a flash, he was attacking his best friend. He grabbed the shocked lad in a head lock and tried to drag him to the floor. "What the fuck are you doing cunt?! screamed Pez. All six of the Skegness F.C fellas intervened to pull the pair apart. The barman stood fixed to the spot, watching this chaotic scene play out in front of him.

The half dozen sportsmen were able to easily drag Rudy outside of Custers' and then out into the street. The guys stood ready for trouble as they let the drunk go. But to their collective relief the intoxicated bar room scrapper seemed to have had enough. He turned on his heels and stumbled away. They watched as he almost came off the pavement and into the road twice as he trudged off into the night.

Waking up the next day in the early afternoon with a total stinker of a hangover, Rudy tried to piece together the events of the previous night.
He couldn't actually remember how he made it back to North Parade. He let himself believe that he could not have been too out of it due to the fact that he was naked and his clothes from the night out at Kush were neatly folded on his wooden chair in the corner of the room.
He paced about the house trying and failing to get a grip on his feelings. The old man must have been out and about.
The kid was angry and unstable. His mind's eye kept pulling him back to the humiliating

scene of his best mate picking him up and lifting him away from the ladies. No forgiving mood was going to wash over him in this state.

His guts were doing a lot of complaining but he managed to force down some tea and toast. Then came some pointed questions as he sat looking out the window at the grey and rainy day. *What am I even doing here right now? I could be anywhere, so why am I sat here? Where do I want to be? How soon can I get there?*

After what had happened in New York he didn't fancy going back to the Big Apple. He didn't fancy America more generally.

Rudy hadn't told anyone about the mugging. At the time it didn't seem like the most major thing. This kind of crap happens to so many people every day he told himself. Of course this was true. But some of the victims dealt with the pain and possible trauma better than others.

It was just one minute out of his life. He took a turn down a street not too far from his hotel (a street he had been past a few times but hadn't walked down until that evening). One moment some scruffy looking little guy with half a cigarette in his mouth is asking him for a light. The next there is a gun in his face.

Back at the hotel, not more than ten minutes after the robbery, Rudy was looking at himself in the bathroom mirror and wondering how he had stayed so calm. He gave no resistance which was smart. He handed over his cheap plastic wallet which only had 30 dollars in it. His bank card was safe in the sock draw.

Little by little that scene started to eat at the kid. *Maybe I could have taken that thieving little cunt. Maybe the gun was a plastic toy?*

The thought of some little piece of shit putting one over on him was something he seemed to have great trouble digesting. He wished maximum harm on his mugger. He hoped nothing but misery would find him.

Unlike last time there would be no face to face goodbyes or any send off.
Based on the conversation that Cyril had with his son the night before he left he would be forgiven for thinking that the kid was A ok. They had a bit of a chat while crashed out in front of the old wide screen. Rudy told him that last night's piss up was a jolly time but he was kind of regretting one drink too many.
His son went to bed first. Cyril stayed up for another couple of hours watching a dark 1970's sci-fi movie he hadn't seen in ages. The middle aged fellow woke up late the next day. He checked his messages and saw

that there was one from Dora and one from his lad. He opened the one from his ex-partner first. She informed him that Rudy had messaged her about an hour ago. He was good enough to let her know that he was on a plane to Berlin. He said he didn't know how long he was going to be gone for but he thought he might travel around Europe for a bit and then, if the mood or desire took him, he might go on to Asia. Cyril checked his message from the boy and saw that it basically confirmed what his ex had just told him. Rudy ended his text to the old man by saying *don't worry so much about me. I'll drop you a line sometime.*

Cyril made a house call to Paxton Fields after he had popped down the pub for a swift pint of cold ale. He found Dora to be in a better mood than he had expected. She and Ravi had obviously been having a laugh about something just prior to his arrival. Even so, Dora said she was concerned about their son. She thought he was keeping things from her and that he might be in a tough place emotionally speaking. Cyril tried to put her mind at ease by talking about the conversation they had had last night but Dora was not convinced and she simply restated her position.

Ravi was good at sensing when it was a good time to redirect the social energy. "I suppose you've heard about all the shit that's gone on at Nutlins then Cyril?" The senior Mr Rudge responded "Yeah mate, pretty fucked up". He didn't sound particularly interested but Ravi pressed on. "I reckon they might have to shut the place down for a while...due to the ongoing investigation". He was referring to the drug bust that had happened just a matter of days ago. It seemed that many Nutlins employees, including those in management positions, had been pushing cocaine and ecstasy around the resort and had made a shit load of cash doing so. But someone had grassed and their lucrative operation had come crashing down. "This is what happens when you get greedy" said Cyril as he put the kettle on. Dora smirked and Ravi rolled his eyes.

Rudy Rudge had plenty of his late uncle's cash left to spend. Would he get to burn it all away or would he crash the plane into the cliff he wondered.

Berlin was fantastic. He couldn't help but compare it to New York and L.A (and it compared very favorably). For the first few days he took it easy and allowed his mood to return to a more even level. The whole Pez thing had pissed him off more than he would have admitted to anyone. But he had ways to sooth and distract his chattering brain.

He arranged to meet an escort calling herself Brandi at her apartment. She lived in a very nice suburb of the German capital. Brandi appeared to be of African decent. She spoke very good English (better than the lad in fact). He would have placed her in her late twenties.

The lady welcomed him into her home with a glass of white wine and gave him a little tour of the gaff. The view of the buildings and streets three stories below were a sight to behold. It was early evening time.

He had chosen Brandi because of what she was offering and because he digged her look. She was a tall woman with a well cut figure. Her eyes were intense.

The game was fairly simple. Her apartment was more than big enough to accommodate the roll play.

With the curtains drawn and Brandi having

gone to hide the game could begin.

Rudy was dressed only in a white thong. In his hand he held a copy of the Bible.

He was in a *dangerous* spot for sure. He had come to this forbidden island in search of a heathen tribe. He was here to try and convert, to try and save the souls of those he encountered.

This missionary didn't have to wait long to find one of the natives. He was confronted by a large woman wearing a leopard skin waist band and not much else. She was not armed. He very much appreciated that she wasn't shaved down below.

She looked at him with a mixture of curiosity and hostility. He would do what he always did. Try to stand firm and preach the good word in the hope that he would reach this sinner's soul. But the native did not understand his words. She just saw an intruder who needed to be dealt with.

Brandi kicked the man-boy right between the legs. That she did not have any footwear on mattered not. The impact sent him crashing onto his back. He let out a pathetic howl. The native didn't let up. She hit him with several more (slightly less brutal) punts into the groin area. He almost passed out.
Brandi dragged the kid across her nice polished floor to her *cave*. There she would finish him off good and proper.

Christmas was approaching but he couldn't have given a fuck about anything less. Europe was a blast to start with. A great time was had in Germania and Bohemia. By the time he did a tour of the Balkans he was overdoing it on the booze, and when he reached Rome he got the feeling that burn out was just around the corner.
He tried to get in contact with Clinton a couple of times but got no reply. He

wondered if his former boss might have just gotten tired of his life. Maybe he was ghosting everyone and taking a mental health break from England.

Rudy had made his way to Asia in early November. As he left southern Europe behind he called his old man, his mum and Gerry. He told them that he was having the time of his life and things could not be any better. His family smelt bullshit of course. Dora could hear in his voice that something was off. Cyril was glad to hear from the boy. They even had a bit of a laugh on the phone talking about some local Skeggy dickheads who had fallen foul of the law. But the old man sensed the same basic thing that Rudy's old dear did. Mr Rudge senior half expected to get a call or text informing him that his son was in trouble with the law (or maybe something worse).

Gerry wanted to keep her brother talking for a good while. She managed to keep him chatting for almost an hour. He even had a few words with Lisa who was very interested in where he was heading. She herself had been to Cambodia. The memory of that trip had not left her. This would have been in no small part to the actual trip on L.S.D she did during one night on the beach with her pals. Gerry told Rudy that he should *take his foot off the pedal* every once in a while, no matter how he felt. She said this was her *big sisterly medical advice*. The young fella simply said that he *heard her*. But she had a feeling he may have to learn a hard lesson.

He had been in the Cambodian capital for a few weeks. It took him a while to find what he was looking for.
The climate was something he had never experienced. It took some getting used to.

He felt like his internal organs had expanded quite a bit. He said to himself that *Asia Rudy was a little bigger and a little slower.* He walked around the busy streets at a more measured pace than he had back in cooler Europa.

He found a group of girls and a seedy and dirty little place that was more than willing to indulge his lurid fantasies. *Was this the bottom of the barrel?* Rudy asked himself. *No, I can go lower.*

His hotel was the kind of place that might be shut down if it were in Europe or North America. He had seen two rats in the shared bathroom and an assortment of freaky looking insects in his own room. It was in this room that he sat on the bed in a sweat soaked t-shirt thinking about his life and such. The kid was coming around to the view that Leonard's death and money were a curse. His gift was cursed coin. What would his life be like now if his uncle was still in the land of living? He would surely still be living the life of *jack the lad* in Skeggy. He would still be working at the Plaza, where the customers respected him and his boss saw him as a decent fella. There would be no distance between him and his loved ones. There would be no ill feeling between him and Pez. They could go riding together. He wouldn't be so alone and he would be blissfully unaware of how large and callous the world really is.

There was still a good chunk of the cursed coin left to spend. He imagined that he would move on to another Asian country, perhaps Thailand, when he was done with this strange Kingdom. But what did it matter where he went? He would be the same impulsive kid with a stiff dick wherever he wound up.

Rudy Rudge had fallen into a trap. It was a trap that many young men before him had fallen into. He had believed that living on the edge and seeking to indulge his desires and whims at every turn would lead him to a state of bliss. But he couldn't have been more wrong. In gratifying his senses and living out his warped dreams over and over he had worn himself down spiritually and brought his mind into a pit of addiction. In order to achieve those cheap and short lived highs that he so craved he needed to engage in more elaborate and extreme games.

The seedy place was the scene of tonight's game. The young English chap showed up in the clothes he had been wearing for the last five days. He was greeted at the entrance by the pimp who ran the establishment. The same guy ran the bar next door.
This was very much the rough part of town.

In places like this western perverts might come looking for young girls or boys. Local criminals were only too happy to help people like that out.

'The one and only' paid the low life in the yellow shirt and purple sunglasses and descended the stairs to the 'dungeon' as he had a few times now. Down here four ladies were waiting for him. One of the women, a bit older than the other three, ordered the man-boy to strip down naked and get in the shower. It was cold water only. She commanded him to wash his cock and balls and the crack of his arse with the little bar of soap he had been provided with. When he was done he stepped out and dried himself off in a casual and none too hurried way. The slightly older lady didn't like what she was seeing. She slapped him hard across the face and commanded him to go down on all fours. They would start by making the kid bark, pant and roll over like a good little doggy. Next they would make him clean their boots. Since he did this so well he would then be made to clean all four of their arse holes while being told to describe how much he was enjoying the privilege. His attempts to speak were met with mocking laughter.

The table in the middle of the 'dungeon' was where he would be pushed flat on his back. Two of the girls would hold his arms out at his sides. One girl got up on the table and squatted over his face. The last lady approached with her well lubricated strap on. She spread his legs and prepared to penetrate. Before she did the woman on the table brought her arse and full weight down on his face. He took in a big sniff of her unwashed pussy. Moments later, as he struggled for air, he felt the plastic phallus pushing into him. The pain and the sense of panic were exquisite. As the thrusting started it only got worse. He would only be allowed little breaks to catch his breath. The fact that the girls who had his arms were digging their fingernails into him made it all the more exciting.

He walked the streets that night on a high. But of course it didn't last long. But 1am he was back in his nasty room, sat on the bed, looking at some brown insect climbing the wall.

As he was starting to nod off he heard his phone ping. He squinted his eyes at the top of the screen and was just about able to make out a message from Gerry. He opened it up and saw that it was two paragraphs of text. He couldn't be bothered to read it all in his tired state but he did notice the bit at the bottom. It said *love u bro. We all do x*
Rudy's heart lifted a little.

He would rise at noon and read the rest of the message from his sister. It was full of the usual good advice. He resolved to give her a call later that day. He was also playing with the idea of calling Pez. Maybe their friendship could be salvaged. He felt there was a chance anyway.

Suddenly there was a commotion outside. Were dogs fighting in the street!? He heard panicked voices amidst the snarling and growling. His impulse was to go and investigate. He put on his smelly t-shirt and his chewing gum white shorts and his beat up trainers. By the time he hit the street though the combatants had been separated and some locals were chasing the canines away with large sticks.

Other works by Steven Forester available

on Amazon in paperback and on Kindle (works of fiction unless otherwise stated).

Adult Short Stories (2020)

Adult Short Stories 2: More Tales for you (2021)

Frank's Jack: A Four Part Novella (2021)

The Great Gant: A Sordid Novella (2021)

Rylee: City at the Hard Edge (2022)

The Christ is Fallible (2022)

Edification Party Manifesto, Philosophy

and Imagination (non-fiction) (2021)

Crisis Diaries: Journals Kept in 2020 & 2022 (non-fiction)

Printed in Great Britain
by Amazon

ISBN 9798367377200